They laid Jessie down by the pond, and Jim bent over her, pushing on her chest. "I can't feel anything. I think she's gone," he said.

Jasper stood silently watching. Matt couldn't speak. Jim held poor Jessie up by her hind legs and let the water stream out of her nose. Then he put his ear to her side and said, "There's just a flicker of life. Fetch something warm to wrap her in, Matt. Hurry!"

Please
Save
JESSIE

by Christine Pullein-Thompson

Cover illustration by Doug Henry

Published in this edition in 1989 by
Willowisp Press, Inc.
401 East Wilson Bridge Road
Worthington, Ohio 43085

Printed in the United States of America
10 9 8 7 6 5 4 3 2

ISBN 0-87406-429-5

One

MOVING men in dark blue overalls were carrying the Painters' furniture into the old farmhouse. There was not much, because for most of their lives they had lived in rented houses or apartments. Matt carried in Jessie's basket, putting it beside the old wood stove before turning to the female black Labrador to say, "This is your home now, Jessie, forever and ever. We're never going to have to move again."

Jessie looked up at his face, her eyes shining, the small white mark under her chin glinting in the autumn dusk.

Matt's mother was holding Jessie's son Jasper, a ten-month-old, gangling black Labrador who had yet to learn manners. He took after his father, a high-strung, stray black Labrador. Jessie had mated with him last winter, when she had been homeless and starving, waiting for Matt or Matt's Uncle Eric to appear and take her home. But now there was a gleam to Jessie's coat again, her ribs were covered with a thin layer of body fat and her eyes were bright and shining. Sometimes it seemed like a miracle to Matt that the terrible weeks when she had been lost were now forgotten—only Jasper remained to remind them of her ordeal.

Jessie climbed into her basket and waited, pathetically anxious to please, as though everything which had happened in the past had somehow been her fault. The look in her eyes made Matt cry, "Don't worry, Jessie, we are never, ever, leaving you again. I promise. Cross my heart."

Matt's father Maurice Painter had taken a cut in salary so that he could settle in East Anglia. Now he represented his company in Holland instead of the United States of America and would be able to commute to work by plane from Norwich. It meant Matt could stay at one school, Mrs. Painter could have a permanent job, and they would at last have a house they could call their own. It had been a sacrifice for Mr. Painter, but he had taken the decision for his family and felt proud of it. This was to be a new beginning for all of them, a period when at last they would be able to put down roots and make friends.

Jessie looked around and liked what she saw—the low-ceilinged, beamed kitchen, the back door which led straight out into a driveway, yard, and farmhouse. Her nose told her that mice had been in the house until recently, that the house had been empty of humans for many months and that soot had fallen down the fireplace. She sensed that Mrs. Painter was anxious and that Mr. Painter was happy in an aggressive way, because like most good salesmen he had an aggressive streak to his nature. She felt that Matt was both excited and happy and she knew that

6

her basket by the stove meant that this was to be her new home.

Jasper was wildly excited. Mrs. Painter had tied him to a post in the yard and he tugged and strained to get away. He wanted to run and run, to dig up the overgrown borders in search of bones and to chase and eat the rabbits which he was certain had been running across the yard a short time ago. His restless eyes searched the dusk as he pulled and choked against the collar which restrained him. Indoors, Matt's mother had found the electric kettle and the one and only electric switch in the kitchen and was making tea for the moving men. Mr. Painter was struggling to fix the wood stove, because fallen soot had made it difficult to light.

Matt wandered outside with Jessie at his heels and found a scattering of leaves on the pond where horses had drunk in the past. In the west the wide open sky was streaked red and gold, with a red autumn sun going down over the horizon. Everything seemed very quiet and still compared with the other places they had lived. It was like leaving a crowded room for an empty one, thought Matt. This place felt as though nothing had really changed in years, and never would. He was wrong, of course, because the countryside is always changing—from open land to enclosures, and back again from winter to spring, from spring to summer, from summer to fall.

But now Matt was almost frightened by the silence as he turned back toward the house, while Jessie ran across the lawn, smelling the rabbits that had been there.

There was a barn by the house and an acre of rough land beyond, where untidy, prickly plants grew higher than Matt's head. They were dying now, but in the summer they had been full of butterflies. An owl hooted high up in a dead elm, and Matt could hear branches creaking in the light breeze. He now realized that the country was not so silent after all—it was simply that he was not yet used to it. But Jessie was catching every sound and smell, and these noises made more sense to her than the London traffic. The new smells were much more interesting to her than the car exhaust and city fumes of London. Matt sensed her happiness, and was suddenly happy, too.

"We'll go for long walks, and you never need to be on the leash again. This whole place will be yours to explore—your property, Jessie. You can make dog friends, and Jasper will become a really good dog, just like you were when you were young. Just you wait, Jessie. You're going to be happier than you've ever been before," he said, as he returned to the house.

After he entered the house, Matt noticed some lights come on down at the end of the lane. His father exclaimed, "Oh, it looks like someone has bought the cottage! I was hoping no one would. I just hope they are our type of people."

Matt began wondering what "their" type of people were like. His mother said, "Let's hope they're helpful, with a couple of nice kids Matt's age, because we're going to need nice neighbors with you being away so much, Maurice."

"I didn't think anyone would be brave enough to

take it on," Mr. Painter said.

Willow Tree Cottage had been for sale when the Painters had first looked at their new home, which was called Willow Tree Farm. Both the old properties were listed, which meant that alterations could not be made without permission from the County Council. Viewing Willow Tree Farm for the first time, Matt's father had said, "That ruined cottage will soon fall to pieces. No one can possibly live in it—there isn't even proper plumbing and the roof's falling in." Because he wanted it that way it had seemed to be a fact. Neither Matt nor his mother had contradicted him, nor had they imagined people ever moving in to share the lane.

They had fallen in love with Willow Tree Farm that summer day, with the sun shining on everything. "There's plenty of room for Jasper and Jessie here, Matt," his mother had told him. "We can keep chickens, too, if you like, or sheep. We can even get a pony, if you want. It'll make up for all those years spent moving about. We'll stay here until you're grown up and married."

"Oh, Mom, that's years away," Matt had answered, but all the same she had made the place sound like paradise.

The moving men were leaving now. "Thank you for your help. We couldn't have done it without you!" Mrs. Painter said as the men left. The movers waved good-bye and drove down the lane and out of sight.

Jessie was in her basket watching Matt. The wood stove was working at last. Matt's mother handed him a can of dog meat and a can opener. "I've put Jasper in the barn, but he needs feeding, Matt," she said.

Matt went out to the barn and gave Jasper meat, a biscuit, and a bowl of water. Jasper ate his dinner in less than ten seconds, then licked Matt's freckled face by way of thanks. "Yuck, Jasper!" exclaimed Matt, wiping his face clean with a handful of straw. "Please be good! This is your home now. I'm sorry you can't be in the house, but you're such a crazy dog, aren't you?" He asked the restless dog. "Here you are, nearly eleven months old and still behaving like a puppy. Will you ever behave? Will you ever stop chewing things? We put you in training kennels because you wouldn't behave, and you cost Dad a fortune. You've got to change, Jasper, for your own sake," Matt finished, and smiled when Jasper held up a large, black paw, as though he was trying to say, "Forgive me."

And that's the trouble with the puppy, Matt thought, as he shut the barn doors. Jasper's both lovable and awful at the same time. You start loving him and he does something terrible, like tearing up your bedspread, and you don't love him any more. If only he could be more like Jessie—a second Jessie.

"Okay. I gave him some water, too," Matt said to his mother as he entered the warmth of the kitchen.

"Is he settling down?" asked his mother, looking at Matt with her steady hazel eyes which so nearly matched her light brown hair.

"Yes, as much as he ever will. He wants to be in here with us, but he can't, can he?" asked Matt.

"No, it's out of the question," she said firmly. "We shouldn't have kept him at all—one dog is enough.

I spend hours picking up Jessie's hairs as it is."

There was a knock at the door and Jessie started to bark, her voice echoing because the house still needed carpets and more furniture.

"It's only us from the cottage. We just came by to see whether you needed any help," a man's voice called.

Matt opened the back door and was confronted by two men, one clean-shaven, the other bearded, both in their thirties. They were dressed in scruffy jeans, T-shirts, oiled jackets and boots, all spattered with paint. Their heads were topped by wool hats, one red, one khaki, and Matt knew at once with a sinking feeling that they weren't what his father called "our sort of people." The taller one, who had a front tooth missing, said, "We live in the cottage. We're fixing it up. We thought we ought to introduce ourselves. This is my friend Reg, and I'm Jim." He bent down to pat Jessie, and Matt could see that his fingers were dirty with plaster.

Matt's father was standing behind Mrs. Painter. He was intelligent, and a handsome man. His mustache was neatly clipped, his hair combed, and his hands were clean. "Living in the cottage? But it must be uninhabitable!" he cried in genuine astonishment.

Putting the kettle on, Matt's mother said, "Come in. Don't stand outside in the cold." The two men kicked off their boots and rubbed their hands together. Matt saw that Reg's hair was blond and curly and that his beard had red in it. His face appeared sharp beneath the wool hat, while Jim's was longer and he had gray eyes. They warmed their hands around mugs of tea while Jessie sniffed their legs.

"We wondered who had bought the cottage. But how are you managing?" Matt's father insisted.

"Fine, no problem. We don't mind roughing it. And the County Council has given us permission to have a camper while we're working on it," Jim said, finishing his tea. Matt had the feeling that Jim would speak for both of them more often than not. Taking his mug to the sink, Jim said, "Well, thanks for the tea. If you don't need any help, we'll be off."

Jessie watched them putting their boots on and wagged her tail uncertainly.

"Thanks for stopping by," Matt's mother said, and the men both turned to smile at Matt before they left, shutting the door quietly after them.

"Just what we didn't want," said Matt's father immediately.

"At least they came to say hello," replied Mrs. Painter.

"But who are they? They don't sound like local people, so why are they here?" Mr. Painter exclaimed.

"Oh, don't be so suspicious!" cried Matt's mother.

"They're unemployed, that's certain."

Matt sat with an arm around Jessie and said nothing. He had liked their new neighbors and Jessie had thought they were okay, and she did not like everyone, not by a long shot. "They seemed okay to me," Matt said. "I mean, they weren't stuck up or anything and they did offer to help—and Jessie seemed to like them as much as she likes anyone the first time."

"Oh, I expect they're all right, Matt. They just aren't the type we want to invite over for dinner," his father said. "We would have liked a couple in business, or the arts, something like that."

"I'm sure they've got hearts of gold," his mother said, smiling down at Matt. "You go ahead and make friends, okay?"

Later Matt lay in bed with Jessie beside him in her basket which he had carried upstairs to his room. His father had wanted her to sleep in the hall, but his mother had objected, saying that Matt needed company. The bed was new, the small window did not have curtains yet, and the ceiling sloped above his head. Matt was glad for Jessie's company, for the room seemed full of ghosts, and the night outside was black and starless, without lights from other houses or passing cars. The silence was overwhelming, but sometimes Matt could hear poor Jasper barking in the barn. It was a lonely sound which made him wish that Jasper could be inside the house with everyone else, but he knew it was impossible because of the dog's habits.

Jasper was so unlike Jessie in every way that it was difficult to believe that they were related, let alone mother and son. Anne, Matt's best friend from London, had said that it was because Jessie had been restless and unhappy when she was expecting Jasper. If he had not been so stubborn and strong, Jasper would have died at birth, like Jessie's other pups.

"He had to be strong, can't you see?" Anne had insisted, staring at Matt. Blond and chubby, Anne was someone who seemed to know all the answers, but whether they were always right was a different story.

The Painters had tried to find Jasper a home. He had even gone to two different owners, first to a family with five children, where he had collided with the stroller and tipped the toddler out. Then he was given to a young man who had wanted a dog to walk with. But when the young man came home from work and found his best suit torn to shreds, he had returned Jasper and threatened to sue the Painters.

Matt's father had wanted Jasper put to sleep after that, but, because of Matt's pleadings, had sent the dog to training kennels where he had apparently learned nothing. Now they were hoping that the countryside would suit him better, for Jasper didn't just chew and tear things to shreds. He also chased cats and motorcycles and cars, rushing along beside them snapping at their tires. And he seemed to be inexhaustible. However far you walked him, Jasper never became tired, and always wanted more of everything. He always wanted more food, more exercise, more fun. When you had just thrown a ball for him for half an hour and walked him for twice as long, he still looked at you with his dancing, impatient eyes asking, "What's next? Where now?" It was almost as though his legs were made of steel! Yet Matt loved him, not as he loved Jessie, because he could never love another dog as he loved her, but with a cooler sort of affection.

Jasper did not only exhaust human beings—he exhausted Jessie, too. Jessie often snapped at him, as if she were saying, "Leave off," or "Grow up." But now she slept, stirring uneasily when an owl hooted, while Matt thought about the future. He was half pleased and half afraid.

This will be forever, he thought, so there's no turning back. Jessie is liking it already and there will be room for Jasper, and we'll see much more of Dad, so it must be better. But he was still not sure about the move, not yet, not until he had been to the local school and walked the dogs across the countryside. A few more days and he would know, but now his fears lingered. One of Matt's dreams turned into a nightmare in which Jessie was on a train disappearing into the distance, while he stood on a long platform in his pajamas calling, "I've lost Jessie! She's on the train. Stop it, please stop it!" But no one moved, and soon Jessie vanished for ever.

Two

WHEN Matt woke up the next day the fall sun was already shining through the window and the sky was grey and pink with shifting clouds. Jessie had left the room. Dressing quickly, Matt found her sitting by the wood stove in the kitchen.

"I let you sleep in because I thought you'd be tired," Mrs. Painter said. "But as soon as you've eaten, please take Jasper out for awhile. He's howling his head off in the barn!"

Matt found some cereal, poured some into a bowl, and added milk. Jessie watched his every move, as she often did. He could hear his father typing in the pantry which he was turning into an office. Matt ate his breakfast quickly and hurried out to the barn. He opened the barn doors and Jasper bounded out and started running in circles, while Jessie looked on.

Reg and Jim were bending over a rusty old car, but they raised their heads as Matt passed with the two dogs. Jim said, "Did you sleep all right?"

"Yes, thank you."

"I bet you found it quiet after London," Jim went on, straightening his back, his pockets bulging with tools.

"Why do you think we came from London?" Matt asked while Jessie sniffed their legs and wagged her tail, which made Matt think that dogs made friends quicker than humans.

"There, and America. It's your voice," Jim said. "You haven't got a local accent."

Matt nodded. "I've lived in so many different places I don't really belong anywhere—not yet anyway," he said.

"You'll never belong here. It takes too long, twenty-five years at least," Reg told him, stooping to pat Jessie.

Matt could see the cottage better now. Recently stripped to its timbers with the roof gone, it looked more like a skeleton than anything else. There was a camper parked next to it, not the kind you see at campgrounds, but an old rusty one with sagging tires. Chickens scratched under it and two overflowing trash cans waited to be emptied. Jasper eyed everything, his mouth watering with hunger, while Reg kicked the car with helpless anger, knowing that they had bought another dud. Then he looked at Matt and saw a boy small for his age, with neat hands, dark hair, and brown eyes, who reminded him of his own two children, now elsewhere with their mother— children whom he had loved and lost through his own foolishness.

"I'll teach you how to drive if you like," Reg said. "You're allowed to drive on a private road, but you must ask your parents first."

"You mean it?" cried Matt.

"Yes, I do."

"Thanks a million!"

"When we've got a car which actually goes," Jim added.

Matt walked on and found a footpath winding along beside a hedge, full of pheasants which soared into the sky at his approach and made Jasper's mouth water. He strained on the leash which Matt had attached to his collar, knowing that if he let him off the puppy might not return until dinner time. Jessie ran ahead, her head down, tail wagging, sending more pheasants wheeling into the sky, and, because Matt was thinking about Reg and Jim and seeing himself driving a car, he did not notice the pheasant hen which rose between Jasper's paws until the next moment, when it was dead.

Horrified, he called Jasper, then looked up and saw a tall man approaching. He was carrying a gun and had a cocker spaniel at his heels. He had a cap on his head and was wearing a leather coat and rubber boots.

Guiltily, Matt pulled Jasper away from the pheasant and with his heart racing like an express train he used his feet in an attempt to cover the bird with grass. But the spaniel had scented her already so there was no escape, and Matt was rooted to where he stood, while the spaniel picked up the pheasant and laid it at her master's feet.

"And who are you, and what are you doing down here with two dogs?" the man demanded, first picking up the pheasant, then dangling it in front of Matt's nose. "You'll have to pay for this, you know."

"I will, of course I will."

"His lordship loses on his pheasants as it is, and it's people like you who put farmers off allowing the public onto their land." He did not talk like a local. "I suppose you're a Londoner," he added rudely.

"I'm not anything really, just British, and I'm very sorry," Matt said.

"People pay lots of money every day to hunt on this land. I will have to tell his lordship. What's your name and where do you live?"

"Painter. Matt Painter, and we live just back there at Willow Farm. We only arrived yesterday. It won't happen again, I promise you."

The man was leaning down to pat Jessie, muttering, "And you're a fine-looking girl, a very fine girl. I wouldn't mind you for myself—you'd make a wonderful hunting dog."

Matt's heart had stopped racing, but he was wondering what his father would say and whether his lordship would call himself. He was worrying already, imagining his father saying, "It's the last straw. Jasper will have to be put to sleep." He wondered whether Jasper would ever learn to behave himself and become like Jessie, and why things were going wrong so soon. Obviously it was his fault, he thought, looking at the ground in embarrassment.

"Keep them both under control in the future," the man continued, standing upright again before slipping the pheasant into a large pocket in his trousers. "Learn the Countryside Code. I know this is a public right of way, but you must keep your dogs under control. Do you understand?"

Matt nodded and watched the man walk back the way he had come, his dog at his heels. He seemed to blend in with the countryside. Matt turned for home. Reg and Jim were still working on their car. They looked at Matt, and, seeing the strain on his face, Jim asked, "All right? Is everything all right?"

"Jasper killed a pheasant, and a man showed up with a gun, and now his lordship is going to call, and my Dad will be so angry. He hates Jasper already." He had not meant to talk to them at all, and here he was telling them everything.

"Don't worry," Jim smiled, showing the gap in his front teeth. "That was Steve, the gamekeeper. He won't tell anyone—he'll take the pheasant home and cook it for his dinner. Don't worry yourself over it. These things are sent to try us."

"He'll never tell Lord Hislop," agreed Reg. "His lordship will be busy in the House of Lords. Besides, you can't count pheasants, so they won't miss one." He held out a piece of chocolate to Matt. "Here, take it, and stop worrying. Just keep little Jasper on a leash next time."

Matt felt better right away, as though a cloud had suddenly been removed from in front of the sun. "So my Dad won't even be told?" he asked.

"Not unless you tell him yourself, of course," replied Reg. And though he did not want to get too friendly with them, because his father would not approve, Matt felt grateful.

"Thanks for the chocolate. How are the repairs

going with the cottage?" he asked, more out of politeness than anything else.

"Fine," said Reg. "Want to see it?"

The next moment they were showing him around, explaining how they were rebuilding everything just as it was before, because it was a historical building.

"Each brick has to be put back as it was, and we'll have to make the windows ourselves because you can't buy the right kind nowadays," Jim explained. They showed him where the stairs would be going up next week and where they planned to put a bathroom.

"At the moment we are waiting for the thatcher to thatch the roof," Jim said. They showed him the garden and the chickens scratching in freshly dug earth. Then they fetched him three chicken eggs, saying, "Have these for your breakfast, Matt." They patted Jasper and said, "He's a nice dog. He just needs a telling off occasionally."

"Thank you for the eggs. I've got to go," said Matt at last.

Jim called after him, "Don't worry, Matt! Everything will be all right. Let sleeping dogs lie."

Reg shouted, "Come and help us anytime, and we'll teach you how to put a car together." Matt could not help liking them, whatever his father said.

He put Jasper back in the barn, which was full of old straw and bales of hay as well as some unwanted kitchen appliances, and he imagined how it must have been with horse-drawn wagons going in and out. He got Jasper some water and decided that he would not tell anyone about the pheasant. He would do as Jim suggested and let sleeping dogs lie. But the decision somehow made him feel closer to Jim and Reg because now they shared a secret and he was a traitor to his parents to whom he had always told everything before.

His mother was surprised to see the eggs. "I hope you said thank you," she told Matt.

"Of course I did." replied Matt. "They want to teach me about car engines and how to drive. That would be helpful, wouldn't it, Mom?" he asked.

She told him to wait for awhile. "We don't really know them yet, do we?" she asked. "They might even be car thieves for all we know."

"Jessie doesn't think so, and she's always right. She likes them," Matt said slowly and wondered why his parents were so suspicious of everybody.

"You start school tomorrow. We had better get your things together, Matt," his mother said.

"Another school," he groaned. "Do I have to go?"

"Yes, you've missed enough school as it is," his mother answered.

In the afternoon a woman appeared towing a large white billy goat. "You don't know me—I'm Janet Hinkley," she said, staring out of a mane of tangled red hair going grey. Then, holding out a lined and battered hand, she added, "I just wondered if you would like Elijah to eat your long grass and weeds. He's much better than any mower."

"He's lovely," exclaimed Matt. "We must have him, Mom!"

"I've brought his chain and stake. He will need to be put in somewhere at night, with a bucket of water, of course," Janet Hinkley continued. "If you can't stand him, bring him back. I live down the next lane on the left. There's a sign saying Ash Tree Farm—that's where I live."

Elijah was wearing a strap around his neck with a rope attached. Janet handed the end to Matt, saying, "If you can't have him he'll go to the butcher for dog's meat. And he's sweet, he really is."

Matt saw that she wore tattered jeans, a grey sweater with a hole in one elbow, and the inevitable rubber boots. She looked exhausted.

Smiling at his mother with what she called his crooked smile, Matt led Elijah away to the rough land beyond the barn. His mother followed, her face creased with worry. She was carrying the stake, a chain, and a hammer, muttering, "I don't know what your father will say. We should have asked him first."

Janet Hinkley called after them, "What a lovely female Labrador! Pity about the white under her chin, but she's a real sweetie, isn't she?"

Jasper was barking inside the barn, as Matt's mother started hammering in the stake. "We can't keep this goat," she said, stopping to rest. "We can't cope with more animals until we've done up the house."

"I'll look after him. I promise," answered Matt, staring at the goat's eyes which were so large and amber, like Jasper's eyes, except that they were larger and calmer and stared at you as though they could see through to what lay inside.

They fetched their only bucket from under the sink in the kitchen and filled it with water. "It was a trick the way she brought him here like that," complained

Matt's mother, putting the bucket of water down within the goat's reach.

"We can always take him back—she said so. Why are you always against everyone, Mom? He's fantastic. Anne will be crazy about him," Matt said.

"They are taking advantage of us, can't you see, Matt? Reg and Jim only have right of access along the drive and they park their old bangers all along it. Janet Hinkley brings a goat and plonks it here. Goodness knows what will happen next. And I must get a job, and who will look after everything then?" asked Matt's mother.

"I will, of course," replied Matt happily. "And you must admit that Elijah is beautiful. He's like something from an ancient scroll, so white and with a beard. I will look after him, I promise."

"He'll chase Jessie, you'll see," his mother said gloomily. She led the way back to the house which was still in a turmoil with the hall still full of moving boxes and suitcases. Matt's father had already left for Holland, and a feeling of winter was in the air, so she knew that the cold weather would be with them long before the central heating was installed. Things were piling up, and it didn't help that Matt had done nothing about getting ready for school. He was spending all his time talking to Jessie and trying to teach her new tricks, instead of sorting through his old school books, finding his pencil case, and seeing that his pens had ink in them. It was as though he did not want to think about school, and was keeping it out of his mind.

"Janet Hinkley and Jessie liked each other, so

Janet must be all right," continued Matt happily, as though the black Labrador with the white patch under her chin was somehow divine.

"Oh, don't be silly, Matt. You know Jessie likes most people," his mother said crossly, staring at him with tired angry eyes. "Really! You're becoming infatuated with that dog."

"At least she's not against people, like you and Dad," Matt retorted.

"We are not against people, Matt, only wary, and Jessie doesn't know everything. After all, she's only a dog," his mother said.

All the same, Matt was up the next morning, getting ready for school. He said good-bye to his mother and Jessie, and walked to the nearest intersection where he waited with a crowd of strangers for the school bus. His mother had wanted to wait with him, but he was afraid that would make him look childish. He could still see her holding a sad Jessie at the end of the drive. Behind them the drive wound its way past Willow Cottage and its piles of junk, and back home to Willow Farm.

Matt had put Elijah out in the field at eight o'clock, and had taken Jasper for a short run which had only whetted the dog's appetite for more exercise. Jessie had wanted to go to school with him, for she was always afraid he might disappear to the United States as he had once before. But now the other people at the bus stop were speaking to him in voices he could not understand and using strange words, and talking about being "crazed." "The headmaster, he crazies you," said a fair-haired boy, while the girls stared at Matt admiringly and blushed when he smiled back.

The school, which was new, was very well equipped, with a new science area and a room full of computers. There were also acres of playing fields and a swimming pool. Students crowded around Matt at lunchtime. He told them about living in the United States and they thought he was an airplane pilot's son. His mind kept straying back to Willow Farm during lessons, wondering whether Jasper was still barking and imagining Jessie waiting for him, her nose pressed against the back door.

Three whole days passed, and the leaves fell off the trees and covered everything with a yellow and orange carpet. Sadly, Jessie watched Matt leave for school each morning and welcomed him back each afternoon with joy. Matt's father returned and asked Reg and Jim to park their cars somewhere else. "You only have access to the drive to come and go, nothing else," he said.

They apologized, saying, "It won't happen again, Guv," but they looked just the same, and Matt was sure that behind their bland expressions they were laughing. They had gotten into the habit of calling his father "Guv" (short for Governor) as a way to tease him for being so strict. Matt didn't like it, but he felt that he could do nothing about it, either.

Elijah had settled in. Wild ducks still swam on the pond and when the shooting season started pheasants appeared, seeking shelter from the guns. Matt had made friends with the gamekeeper's son, whose name was Martin. He was an outsider too, having been born outside of the area. A girl named Sharon, with a sharp face and grey eyes, sometimes stopped by, saying that she wanted to feed Elijah. And they all walked the dogs together, with Jasper on a leash and Jessie surging ahead. With the golden leaves everywhere, the dark fields and the red sunsets, sometimes it seemed like paradise.

Matt's father bought Matt a bike and soon he and Martin were riding together on weekends, sometimes taking Jasper, sometimes Jessie, on a leash with them, pedaling along old pathways, where they met no one. Though Jasper could never be Jessie, Matt grew fonder of him, and life might have gone on as pleasantly as that forever if Reg and Jim had listened to Matt's father, and a chicken had not been killed.

Afterward Matt was to look back on those few days as a lull before the storm, a time when everything seemed just right, when even school was bearable. But in spite of letters and polite requests, Reg and Jim continued parking their old bangers along the drive and their chickens roamed freely, digging up the few plants Matt's father had planted in the vegetable garden he was making beside the barn. On weekends Reg and Jim entertained friends who drank straight from wine bottles and laughed loudly, sometimes even spitting onto the grass beside the drive, which was not theirs and to which they only had access. And sometimes when they were working on the old cars they bought and sold to make a living, they would have a radio on full blast. This drove Matt's father into a frenzy, so that soon Matt could only feel relaxed when his father was away.

Added to this, the pair were always doing what Matt's father called scrounging. In particular they seemed determined to acquire the kitchen units in the barn. "They are not doing any good there, Guv," they insisted. "You'll never use them. We'll give you a good price, Guv."

But Matt's father refused to sell them anything, not even things he did not want and for a good price, for he loathed them. They had none of the virtues he admired, because in his eyes they were scroungers, ill-educated and untidy, and most of all because of the mess they were making less than a hundred yards from his own house.

In spite of the angry letters Mr. Painter sent them, the two men continued talking to Matt. They offered him chocolate and sweets, stopping work to pat the two dogs or to help him pull an unwilling goat into the barn for the night. Because Matt's father disliked them, Matt tried to dislike them too, but failed. And Jessie still felt the same about them, welcoming them with wagging tail whenever they met. She did not know that the old cars should not be parked along the drive, that wine should be put in glasses before being drunk, that radios should be played quietly, and that spitting was a dirty habit.

Each time Mr. Painter returned from abroad he seemed to be seeing it for the first time—the skeleton cottage still without a roof, the camper with belongings piled outside, the cars in various stages of repair, the heaps of gravel and cement ready for work which never seemed to happen. Even an old canoe thrown carelessly behind the cottage annoyed him.

"They never make any progress," he fumed. "It's just an eyesore. How can I ask friends to come here when they have to pass that mess? I ask you. How can I?"

Matt's mother could neither soothe nor console him. It was no use telling him that life changed like the wind, for he had heard it all before. It was no use when Jessie welcomed him like a long lost traveler when he returned home. Wherever he went, the mess at the end of the drive traveled with him in his imagination.

Jim and Reg still kept sending messages to him via Matt. "Tell the Guv we will clean everything up by next week and all the cars will be gone. Tell him that the thatcher will be starting on Tuesday and then we can move in. Tell him the sand will be gone by Monday."

Nothing ever happened, so soon Matt stopped passing on the messages. But it was something else which made Reg and Jim very angry, and suddenly made them believe that Jessie should be either tied up or put away.

Three

MATT still liked Reg and Jim, which is what made it all seem so much worse and gave him nightmares afterward. He loved sitting in their old cars, with Jessie in the back, pretending that they were going somewhere exciting. Once Jim had let him drive to the road and back. Sometimes they asked him to run the engines while they peered at the carburetors. They even let him start the mini concrete mixer they had rented, and sometimes he sat in the camper with them playing cards, though he never told his parents this. If Matt had not been so much on his own at this time, with only his mother for company, and she was usually busy, he might not have grown so fond of Reg and Jim. As it was, unless Martin or occasionally Sharon appeared, he was mostly alone after school and on weekends, except for the dogs. Although Jessie was his best friend, she could not teach him about cars and concrete mixers.

Often he would take all the animals out together, but Elijah was obstinate and Jasper never tired, and he always returned exhausted. It was then that Reg or Jim would call, "Would you like a cup of tea?" and Matt would look around guiltily to see whether his mother was looking, before calling, "Okay. Thanks." He told himself that his mother had never forbidden him to talk to the two men and that only his father disliked them. He would put Jasper and Elijah in the barn and rush to join them.

Inside the camper there were always chocolate cookies to eat, while Reg and Jim would crack jokes and ask him about school, recalling their own school days. The camper would be full of fun and laughter, whereas his own home was still in the process of being decorated. His mother was working nonstop in an effort to get everything done in time for Christmas. Jessie enjoyed those tea times just as much, sitting with her head on Matt's knee and hoping for pieces of the chocolate cookies.

"Old Jasper will never be the dog she is. You can see she's one in a million, Matt. Why, she seems to understand every word you say," Reg would say, leaning on the table with both elbows showing through his sweater. And Jim would laugh, saying, "Give old Jasper a chance. He's still not much more than a puppy."

They kept their wool hats on indoors, which Matt's father would have considered bad manners, and the mugs they drank from were not very clean. They still sent Matt home with messages for his father. They said something like, "Tell the Guv, we're sorry about the cars still being there. Tell him they're up for sale and when they're gone we won't be getting any more." But Matt could not pass on the messages because his father had told him not to speak to them.

He did not realize that they disliked his father too, that it had become mutual. He thought they were amused by Mr. Painter's constant complaining notes, written on elegant headed paper. "Just the Guv playing up again," they would say. Nothing appeared to worry them—not their drains overflowing into the drive, or the thatcher never arriving, or the cars rusting away unsold. They seemed to find life a joke, which was why they were such good company. Matt thought they liked him as much as he liked them. He imagined that only his father could fume and rage. He thought that Reg and Jim felt no anger, not with him nor with his parents, and certainly not with Jessie and Jasper.

It was a foggy Saturday when it happened, the air so damp and raw that it seemed to eat into your bones. Matt had let Jessie out first thing in the morning. The postman had come, and the Painters were eating breakfast. Mr. Painter was just cracking the top of a freshly boiled egg, when there was a knock on the door and Reg and Jim burst in. Without taking off their boots or even wiping their feet they started to shout, "Look what your dog has done. Just look!" and they swung a dead chicken hen under Mr. Painter's nose, their faces red with rage. "And she didn't do it on your land, Guv—she did it on ours. We saw her, Guv. We saw her do it!" shouted Reg.

"She was our best egg layer, our best hen. Now who's talking about bad neighbors?" shouted Jim, his eyes bulging.

Matt was on his feet now, shouting, "Not Jessie.

Jessie would never do a thing like that. It's a mistake, I know it is!"

"Did you see her doing it?" asked Matt's father, standing up.

"Yes, Guv, with our own eyes. We took the chicken right out of her mouth."

And there was Jessie standing in the doorway holding up a paw and she looked guilty. Whenever she heard people shouting her name she always felt guilty.

"Jasper might, but not Jessie, Dad," cried Matt. "Jasper knows how to kill. I can't tell you how, but he does."

But now his father pushed him aside and the back of his neck was red with anger. No one could ever stem his anger except Mrs. Painter, so Matt turned to her now, shouting, "Mom! Do something, please, Mom. Stop him!"

"Wait a minute, Maurice," said Mrs. Painter. "There may have been a mistake. It might have been Jasper, but not Jessie."

"What mistake? They saw her with their own eyes," cried Matt's father, seizing poor frightened Jessie by her collar. "And now she's going to get the hiding of her life. I must do it now so that she knows what it's for. Another minute and it will be too late."

"It was Matilda, our best hen," said Reg. "She was the only one still laying. She was a lovely hen."

Matt recalled that they loved their chickens almost as much as he loved Jessie, but still he ran after his father crying, "Don't, Dad, don't beat Jessie!"

Bewildered as she was, Jessie was now expecting

33

a beating, though it had never happened to her before. In a strange way she was sure she deserved it, because humans were her gods and gods don't make mistakes. Whether she had killed the chicken or not, she had somehow done wrong and must be punished for it.

Jasper was howling as though he knew what was about to happen. Matt caught up with his father and, grabbing the back of his coat, cried, "Don't beat Jessie, please don't, Dad. There must have been a mistake because she never even looks at the chickens as we go past. Honest, Dad."

Reg and Jim were walking back to their camper silently with their heads down, carrying their dead chicken.

"They saw her do it, Matt. Isn't that enough? And now she's done it once, she'll go on doing it. Is that what you want, Matt—a killer dog? Then Jasper will copy her and we'll have two killer dogs on our hands. I'm doing it for her own good, Matt. Try and understand," his father said, threading twine through Jessie's collar before tying her to a post in the barn, saying at the same time, "Shut the doors, Matt."

Matt's heart felt as heavy as lead, while his legs felt weak as he closed the heavy barn doors. "You're making a mistake, Dad—I know you are," he said.

But his father was already taking off his belt. Jessie looked at Matt as if to say, "I'm sorry. I didn't mean to do it," and Matt found his face wet with tears.

Meanwhile Jasper ran around and around in circles barking wildly, not sure whether the whole scene was a game or not. Matt knew that Jasper would have taken the beating, simply shaking himself afterward as though saying, "Well, that's over then," but Jessie was different. Jessie was faithful and always did her best. Jessie's heart would be broken, her spirit gone.

Matt's father hit Jessie six times with his belt, which was only made of plastic, and each stroke hurt him too, and so each became less of a blow. But Matt did not know that. He simply saw him beating the dog he loved, and was furious with him because of it. Then his father put on his belt again and took Matt's arm saying, "Come on, cheer up, it's not the end of the world. Don't give her any dinner tonight. She must be punished properly, or it will be Lord Hislop's pheasants next time, and then the keeper will put a bullet through her head."

Matt remembered again how Jasper had killed a pheasant and nothing had happened, but didn't dare mention it to his father. Instead he said, "You beat Jessie because you hate Reg and Jim having one up on you. You didn't have to beat her."

His father retorted, "Oh, Matt, grow up, will you," but he did not deny it, because in a small way it was true. "The thing is done. I didn't like to do it, but I don't think Jessie will kill another chicken." He went back to the kitchen and stood with his back to the wood stove.

"Did you have to do it in front of Matt, Maurice? You know how he feels about Jessie," asked Mrs. Painter as Matt ran through the kitchen and upstairs to his room, slamming the door after him.

Later his father knocked on the door saying, "You're not to go near Jessie for the time being. Do you understand, Matt?"

Matt answered in a stifled voice, "Yes, but what about Jasper?"

"I'll take care of Jasper. We are all going out. We want to go to the store to get some things for the house. Be ready in half an hour," his father said.

"I don't want to go," Matt said.

"You'll do as you're told. Wash your face and put on your coat, and no arguing," replied his father as he went down the stairs with heavy steps, thinking that soon he must order the Christmas turkey.

"It's nearly Christmas. What would you like, Matt? What about a speedometer so you can see how fast you're going on your bike?" Mr. Painter asked later, as he drove carefully past three chickens. "That's what we'll get you, and a set of lights. How about it, Matt? What do you think?"

Matt would not answer at first, but then he said, "I would like Anne to come and visit, please. When can we have her?" He knew she would understand his feelings, because she had been with him before in his darkest hour and because she, too, loved Jessie.

"We'll write," replied his mother, turning to smile at him. "But I don't think she will be able to come until the Christmas holidays."

They parked the car. Then Matt followed his parents around the town which was crowded with shoppers. People jostled each other in a frenzy of shopping, saying things like, "Only five weeks to Christmas," and "I think we'll have beef for a change come Sunday." Small children's hands scrabbled in bags of candy. A toddler sat in a stroller nibbling at a bar of chocolate, dribbling it down her pink coat. A dog sat tied outside a butcher shop. Matt did not want a speedometer, nor lights for his bike. He refused to look at them, and remained aloof, which angered his father.

"Okay, then. Go without," his father said at last, storming out of Woolworth's.

But Christmas had not entered Matt's mind yet, so the threat meant nothing to him. His mind was still with Jessie in the barn. Christmas belonged to another world, wholly separate from the present time. Christmas was something bright in the distance, which might or might not happen.

Matt's parents bought a new electric stove which was to be delivered the next week. They also ordered two armchairs and a bed for the spare room. They bought saucepans and a pair of kitchen scissors, and some curtain material for the front windows. Then they found a restaurant and had lunch. All the time Matt said nothing, so his mother told his father to ignore him. "He'll come around with time," she said.

Matt ate his lunch slowly without tasting any of it. He had made up his mind that he would see Jessie despite what his father had said. He would sneak out in the dark and feed her the bits of his lunch which he was now putting into a paper napkin under the table, bits of hamburger and roll.

"I will have to give them compensation for the hen," announced Mr. Painter as he led the way out of the restaurant.

"You mean Reg and Jim?" Matt's mother asked.

"Of course. Who else? I'll give them twice as much

as they paid for that hen—then they can't say they haven't made a profit out of it. It's obvious that they have no money," his father said.

No one answered and Matt, looking at his mother, saw the strain on her face. They drove home in silence. The murkiness had gone. Sunlight lit up the yard, the dumped cars, the chickens, and the tiled roof of the barn from which no sound came. Matt wondered whether Jasper was comforting Jessie, lying beside her and licking her poor back.

"Still not speaking, eh, Matt?" his father asked, getting out of the car.

And his mother said, "Cheer up, Matt. She'll get over it. Dogs aren't human, you know."

"No, just a thousand times better," muttered Matt, walking indoors without looking at either of them. The hamburger was bulging in his pocket, and ketchup had stained his jeans.

"She'll be just fine tomorrow," his mother said.

"She'll never be the same again, never, never, never—and you know it!" Matt cried.

His father looked at him, and, seeing the stain on his jeans whipped out the hamburger. "So that's what you were up to. All that money for lunch and you put it in your pocket for the dog." He laughed and his laughter appeared worse than his anger because it seemed to make fun of Matt's unhappiness and Jessie's disgrace.

Then Mr. Painter threw the hamburger on the wood stove's fire, and said, "That way nobody will have it, Matt. Now just forget about Jessie. Have a game of cards with me or watch the television. There's soccer on at three o'clock."

But Matt ignored him and went to his room and wrote to Anne. It was a long letter, which ended, *We all need you—me, Jasper and most of all Jessie. Love, Matt.* Putting everything into words made him feel better so that he could see everything more clearly, and he could almost understand his father's actions. He had done it for the best, hoping to teach Jessie a lesson once and for all. It was not right in Matt's eyes, but a necessary action in his father's eyes.

"It must have been Jessie," Mrs. Painter said to Matt later as he stood watching her making curtains in the spare room. "A normal dog would have eaten the chicken, but she's a gun dog, so she just carried it," she explained.

Matt did not answer, for he was imagining Anne's arrival. He imagined Jessie welcoming Anne, with the bad times over, everything all right again.

"We'll make this room nice for Anne. You'll help me, won't you? You can paint the baseboards," suggested his mother.

"I wish she was arriving tomorrow," Matt said.

Later, when his parents were watching television he crept outside and, after opening the heavy barn doors, threw his arms around Jessie. She licked his face over and over again, while Jasper watched, longing for a game. Matt fetched them both some water. It was dark outside now, a winter's night with everything suddenly crisp with frost. He covered Jessie with hay and apologized for having no food to give her.

He left Jessie lying comfortably and slipped

through the big barn doors again. Jim stood outside holding a dish of scraps. "This is for Jessie and Jasper. I'm so sorry, Matt. We didn't want Jessie beaten. We were just upset, that's all. If we had known the Guv was going to take his belt to her we would never have said anything," he said, his grey eyes searching Matt's face.

"She deserved it. Dad was right," replied Matt loyally, though the words stuck in his throat. "And I can't take whatever it is you've brought because Jessie must be punished. Can't you understand?" he continued, his voice breaking with emotion.

"Yes, you can. You can take it for Jessie's sake. She's been punished enough," replied Jim, holding out the dish. Feeling like a traitor torn apart by two loyalties, to Jessie and to his father, Matt took the dish into the barn and shared the food equally between Jessie and Jasper, his flashlight showing them the food as they ate. Jessie looked gingerly at each morsel before eating while Jasper seized it with hungry gulps, not seeming to taste it at all. Matt thought that he seemed more like a wolf than a dog, a killer by instinct, a dog who could take intense heat, or freezing cold, as tough as a husky dog. Then he closed the big doors again, put the bar across them, handed the plate back to Jim and muttered a quick "Thank you" before running back to the house. As he ran, he longed for Anne to arrive because she would know what to do and would sort out right from wrong. She was old for her age and confident— someone he could trust, someone who would keep a secret no matter what happened.

Half an hour later Mr. Painter relented and let Jessie out. She ran straight to Matt and would not look at Mr. Painter. She lay all night in her basket beside Matt while he dreamed that Reg and Jim were killing their chickens themselves one by one. "Now Jessie will never be beaten again," Reg said, smiling at Matt.

Four

ANNE wrote back:
  Dear Matt,

  Granny says I can stay with you from the first day of the Christmas holidays, but I must be back by Christmas. Please ask your mother to call Granny and arrange it. I can't wait to see Jessie again. Is Jasper as wild as ever or is he calming down? Granny won't let me bring little Kim. She says she really needs him as a guard dog—you know how London is! Thank goodness there are people downstairs in the other apartment to keep an eye on Gran. Mom and Dad are abroad again, so I'm spending all my time with Gran now. Poor Jessie, the beating must have been a real shock to her. And now you say she's scared of your father. Jim and Reg sound interesting, and the house sounds really nice. I can't wait to see it all. I've been acting in the school play. It's been so much fun.

  Love,
  Anne

Matt read the letter twice. Several days had passed since Jessie's beating and, except for avoiding Matt's father, she seemed normal. The plumbers were in the house installing the central heating system, only leaving to eat their lunch in the barn at noon and to return to their homes at five o'clock each evening.

Reg and Jim had sold two of their cars and the thatcher had at last arrived to put a roof on Willow Cottage. The weather was becoming colder all the time and people were talking about a long, hard winter. A load of logs arrived and Matt helped his mother to stack them into the old shed which stood next to the house.

Christmas vacation began, and Anne was expected to arrive the next day. Matt hoped she had not changed, for he felt closer to her than to anyone else his own age. Martin and Sharon often came over. Sharon loved Elijah and wanted a pony just as Anne had once, but except for school and the animals Matt had nothing in common with them. They did not know any answers and Matt wanted someone who did, who would say "You were right to put Jessie before your father" and "Of course, you must go on talking to Jim and Reg." He needed someone who would stop him from feeling guilty.

Matt's father had tried to make amends. He gave Matt a small patch of garden as his own, made fusses over Jessie, and he even took Jasper out for a long walk one Sunday afternoon. Recently Matt had forgotten his father's difficult side and thought him nearly perfect.

At last Matt and his mother were waiting on a railway platform to meet Anne, the wind whipping their faces and turning their hands white with cold. The train was late, and the platform became deserted.

But they continued to wait. Jessie waited too, standing meekly beside Matt. She was not a young dog any more, but not old either. Rather, she was in the prime of life, but wise beyond her years because of her past experiences.

"I wish Anne would arrive. Why is the train late, Mom? I'm freezing," complained Matt.

"It's a slow train. She had to change at Ipswich. It won't be long now."

At last the train came into view, a small train with hardly anyone on it. Anne leapt out, kneeling down and throwing her arms around Jessie first of all. "She hasn't changed. She's just the same old Jessie," she cried before kissing Matt's mother. She hadn't changed herself. She was the same fair-haired Anne— always threatening to lose weight but never managing it, always making the best of things, always liking and generally being liked. The very sight of her raised Matt's spirits and drove away his guilt feelings.

"*You* haven't changed, Matt," she said, taking in his freckled face, his upturned nose, his dark hair, and brown eyes. She was wearing a dark blue school overcoat, a jumper, and short fashionable black boots.

She saw Matt looking at her boots and laughingly said, "It's all right. I've brought my rubber boots, too!" She felt as though she was miles away from

London, almost in a different world.

They piled into the car to head home. "Where's Jasper?" asked Anne.

"We can't take him in the car—he's too wild," replied Matt's mother as she started the engine.

"I'll train him. I'll whip him into shape, Mrs. Painter," cried Anne enthusiastically.

"You don't know what you're getting yourself into!" Matt said.

"Did Jessie *really* kill a chicken? It sounds much more like Jasper to me," Anne remarked.

"Jasper was in the barn. Those hooligans next door saw Jessie do it," replied Mrs. Painter.

"You can't call them hooligans, Mom," said Matt.

"Vandals, then."

Anne decided not to be drawn into the conversation. She hated unpleasantness. She could feel the friction between Matt and his mother and wanted to make up her own mind about Reg and Jim.

Jessie was lying with her head on Anne's knee. She never forgot someone who had been kind to her, and Anne had helped Matt rescue Jessie from being drowned as a young puppy.

Anne was staring out of the window now, seeing the treeless landscape and the acres of ploughed hills which were no longer white as the frost thawed. They drove through the village and turned left down the lane, past Willow Cottage which was now three-quarters thatched. Bricks were beginning to fill the gaps between the timbers, and a leafless willow tree was bending over what had once been a lawn. Two old cars were parked outside, one with the hood up.

Then they came to the farmhouse, and Anne exclaimed, "Oh, it's lovely—really nice, Mrs. Painter!"

The sun was shining. Suddenly Matt saw it all through Anne's eyes, comparing it with her home in London. He recalled the constant hum of traffic, the people passing the windows all day long, and the cars parked against the curb. It was so much more peaceful here, and he was glad for her sake that Anne had come, even if it was only for a visit.

They took Anne's luggage to her room, and she loved it at once. "It's so pretty!" she said.

"The central heating is not connected yet, so I've put an electric heater next to your bed. Turn it on whenever you like, Anne," said Mrs. Painter.

"Thank you. It's so lovely here," Anne answered.

"It's wonderful to have you with us, Anne," replied Matt's mother, giving her a hug.

As Anne looked out the window, she saw the fields, the church, and the roofs of cottages. "It's so calm. I never thought anywhere could be so quiet," she said.

Soon Anne and Matt were outside and running into the barn, and they took Jasper for a walk in the winter sunlight. They went along the drive and watched the thatcher at work. They saw Jim and Reg. The men came over to pat Jessie and Jasper, and to meet Anne.

"You must be Anne," said Jim.

"Yes," said Matt. "Anne, this is Jim and this is Reg."

They greeted one another, and then Matt and Anne continued on their way to explore the village. Matt said, "We're not supposed to be friends with them. Dad doesn't like them."

"They seem all right," Anne answered. "They don't seem like hooligans or vandals. You should see some of the people in London!"

"You talk to Dad. He likes you. Please, Anne, tell him to stop hating them!"

"Talk to your father? But I hardly know him!"

"Please. He might listen to *you*."

"I'll try, but I'm not hopeful," she said.

He introduced her to Sharon and Martin, but only Anne could think of anything to say. They made Jasper heel by holding a small stick in front of his nose and then rewarding him with biscuits.

They were home in time for tea. Jasper went indoors with them and, because Anne was there, he was allowed to stay with them for a little while. They ate crumpets dripping with butter, while Jasper watched them, his mouth watering.

"Jasper's eyes are like Elijah's," cried Matt. And then they remembered that the goat was still tethered out in the cold.

"It's such a change after London!" Anne exclaimed, following Matt outside. "And I love Elijah—I really do. You're so lucky, Matt. You don't know how lucky you are—two dogs, and a goat. I don't have any animals I can call my own, not even a gerbil."

Elijah was in a hurry to be inside. The grass was already crisp with frost again after the short thaw. Anne and Matt led Elijah into the barn, and hurried back to the house.

Mr. Painter was back now, thawing out in the kitchen, grumbling that the central heating installation had yet to be finished. He told them that Reg and Jim had flagged him down in the drive.

"They've got some nerve. They are still after those kitchen units in the barn," he said, and explained to Anne that the units had been left by the previous owners of Willow Farm. "I must say those two in Willow Tree Cottage know a bargain when they see one, and I had to agree to sell the units to them," he finished with a hint of admiration in his voice, so that Matt thought that there might be a time soon when they could all be friends.

Matt's mother told them that she had been offered a share in an antique shop. "It's called *Just Your Luck*. If you need something old we try to find it— it may be an old copper preserving pan, or some wooden shoe trees, or a set of chairs. Anything, really. We'll be selling old pictures and prints too," she explained, her face alight with enthusiasm. "It's such a coincidence running into Candy, just when she needed a partner, and she's living near here, too. I just can't believe it! I'm so happy I could cry. I'm starting after Christmas, and I simply can't wait. That is, as long as it's all right with you, Maurice and Matt."

"As long as you don't lose money, darling," said Mr. Painter. "It sounds perfect for you!"

"I think it's really nice," said Anne.

"I'm arranging for Will to come in most days, Matt, so you won't be alone if I'm kept late. You know Will, don't you?" she asked.

Matt knew Will all right—an old man with only one tooth left in his head, who kept cream cakes in the bag on the back of his bike for Jessie. He had worked at Willow Tree Farm thirty years ago when it was still a proper farm, though without electricity or a water supply, just a pump in the back yard.

"I don't need anyone. I'm not a baby anymore," Matt said.

"Well, the animals may need him. He can bring Elijah in and let Jasper out for his run. Please don't be so defensive, Matt," replied his mother.

Reg and Jim were to fetch the kitchen units later in the evening. Matt heard his father telling them to put their cigarettes out before entering the barn. "There's hay and straw in there and you can't be too careful," he finished.

"That's all right, Guv." Reg replied, his small eyes smiling beneath his wool hat. "Don't you worry, we'll see that everything's all right. Do you want cash, Guv?"

"I don't mind, whatever is the easiest," replied Mr. Painter.

"It'll be cash then, easier all around," said Jim.

Matt and Anne were in the sitting room which was next to the kitchen. Matt's mother had papered the walls and painted the doors. There was a picture of Scotland hanging above the fireplace, lots of easy chairs, and a piano which Mr. Painter played sometimes. So everything was taking shape and becoming a home. Mr. Painter had installed a filing cabinet, his desk, and a swivel chair in the old pantry which he was converting into his office. Whenever they had a chance, the two dogs lay at Matt's and Anne's feet, though Jasper was never still for long.

Later that evening Anne telephoned her Grandmother, telling her that she was all right and having a wonderful time. Later still, Reg and Jim knocked on the back door to say that they had taken the kitchen units from the barn. Matt's father kept them on the doorstep talking and Matt could see the glow of their cigarettes as they handed his father an envelope containing money and said, "It's all there, Guv, and we didn't smoke inside the barn. We shut the doors tightly."

It felt late but it was actually only eight o'clock and the workmen were not long gone, having hoped to finish putting the radiators in upstairs before the weekend. Matt's father shut the back door saying, "That's that then. Perhaps those two will stop bothering me now."

He put his hand on Matt's shoulder and said, "Put Jasper out soon, or he'll wreck something. Switch off the outside light before you go to bed, too. You left it on last night."

Matt and Anne went outside with Jasper. It was a very still night with a sky as black as ink.

"It's so dark, but I don't feel frightened. It's funny, because in London I'm always frightened at night, even when everything is lit up," Anne said.

Elijah was eating hay in his pen and they left Jasper loose with a bowl of water and a pile of dog biscuits. Afterward Anne was to say that she had noticed a strange smell in the barn, but she said nothing at the time and Matt did not notice anything unusual. He said, "Now the units have gone we don't need to tie Jasper up any more. It seems so cruel, but Dad was afraid he would chew them."

"I suppose being tied up is okay if the chain's long enough," replied Anne, who was inclined to stand up for Matt's father, seeing the tiredness on his face which Matt did not notice. "Have you noticed your father is going grey?" she asked as they walked back to the house.

"He *is* nearly forty, and that's quite old," replied Matt. "He may be taking us to see a castle tomorrow, or shopping."

"That will be really nice," Anne said. "I wish I had your Dad as a father. I hardly ever see mine."

"Dad would be all right if he wasn't always carrying on about school, or Reg and Jim," Matt said.

"I expect he thinks it's for your own good," Anne said.

"But he keeps changing his mind; one minute he was not selling those kitchen units, and the next he was. He's like the weather these days—always changing," grumbled Matt, going into the kitchen.

Much later that night Matt woke up. He could hear Jasper barking in the barn and Jessie was crying at his door, but there was no light coming through the curtains, which meant it was still night.

"Shhh, Jessie. Go to sleep. You know Jasper—he likes hearing his own voice," Matt said. But now Jessie was on his bed whining and licking his face, then running to the door and scratching at it. Matt found shoes and his bathrobe, switched on some lights, and stumbled downstairs.

"I suppose you want to go to the bathroom," Matt told Jessie, still half asleep, wanting only to return to bed and fall asleep again. Jasper's barking was louder now and there was a funny smell outside which made Matt begin to panic. His heart started beating faster and faster, and alarm bells began ringing in his head.

He flung the back door wide open and almost at once could see smoke emerging from the barn, not flames yet, just billowing smoke. Then he began shouting, "Wake up, everyone, wake up! Fire! Fire! Help! Dad, Mom, the barn's on fire!" He switched on all the outside lights and then he was running toward the barn shrieking, "Jasper, Elijah, don't panic! I'm here. Hang on!"

Five

FEAR and cold made Matt's hands clumsy so that at first he could not open the barn doors. As he struggled he was imagining Elijah choking to death inside his pen, which was fenced by wood and would burn like kindling. He could hear Jasper scratching and whining on the other side. The smoke billowing through cracks in the door made him cough, his eyes were smarting, and he was still all alone in the cold, dark yard.

Finally Matt opened the barn doors, and Jasper rushed out like a whirlwind. Matt was about to enter the barn when his father rushed out and held him back. "Matt, you can't go in there! It's much too dangerous!" he said.

"But Elijah is still inside," Matt cried. "He'll be burned to death!" Then he began to scream, "Elijah, Elijah!"

Anne and Mrs. Painter had joined them, and they too frantically began to call the goat. "Come on, Elijah, come on!" they shouted.

But their calling seemed futile, for Elijah did not

come out of the barn.

Flames began to crackle, and Matt was devastated. "Oh, I wish we could have saved poor Elijah...poor Elijah, he's dead!" he said, and he began to cry.

They heard a racket coming from inside the barn. "It sounds like the pens are breaking up from the fire," Mr. Painter said.

As he finished speaking, Elijah suddenly ran out the barn doors, terrified. He had somehow gotten out of his pen, and he was safe!

"Elijah!" Matt cried. "You're alive—"

"Oh, yes!" Anne said. "He is alive, and he doesn't look like he's even hurt."

Elijah's fur was gray from the smoke, but he was otherwise unhurt. Matt and Anne began to move toward the frightened goat, but Elijah began to run down the drive.

"He'll be okay," Mr. Painter said. "He's afraid of the fire, and his instincts are telling him to get away from it. He'll come back, kids. Don't worry, he won't go far."

At that moment, Reg and Jim appeared with a long hose which they had connected to their outside tap. Then Will arrived, calling, "We need a chain of people with buckets," and started fetching water from the pond.

Matt kept thinking about the animals, knowing that they were safe.

Jim and Reg directed their hose onto the burning sacks and Will threw water over the hay bales near the door, saying, "They won't burn now."

"The fire engine is on its way, but it doesn't look

bad inside," Mrs. Painter said. Come indoors, Matt, love. You've been fantastic. You and Jessie deserve medals," his mother said. "But however did it start?"

Meanwhile Reg and Jim were muttering, "Good thing we got our kitchen units out in time."

Then Matt was saying, "It's all right, Mom, it was only sacks burning. Jessie saved the day because she woke me. Where are Elijah and Jasper? We must find them—Jasper, Jas, Jas, Jasper," he started to call. The smoke was thicker and denser now, but there were no more flames. Only the choking black smoke nearly as black as the night beyond the flashlights and outdoor lights remained.

A fire engine arrived, loaded with tall firemen who connected their hose to a pipe at the end of the drive, uncoiling it automatically. Watching these silent men who knew their job so well, Matt thought that he would like to be a fireman when he was older.

"Anything inside?" one asked.

"No, they're all out." Matt said.

"That's all right then."

Now Matt took his father's flashlight and went down the drive in search of Elijah, Jessie at his heels. These days Jessie was always at his heels, making him feel like her protector. He found Elijah grazing at the roadside, quite unconcerned. But there was no sign of Jasper.

The fire was almost out when he rejoined the others, dragging a reluctant goat. The firemen were wetting everything down with their hoses. His father was blaming Jim and Reg, saying that he expected damages from them. "You were smoking in there. I know you didn't put your cigarettes out, in spite of all I said!" he shouted.

"That isn't true, Guv," answered Jim. "We put our cigarettes out before we entered the barn. I promise we did."

"That's right, Guv," agreed Reg, looking gaunt in the lights from the fire engine. "We would never go in there with our cigarettes lit up."

But they had no one to give evidence, no proof, and now Matt's father was demanding massive damages from them. He was promising them a letter from his insurance agent the very next day and threatening to ruin them, to kick them out of the place. Matt wanted to interrupt, but what could he say? He had no proof either. All the same he pulled at his father's sleeve, saying, "It wasn't them, Dad, I know it wasn't."

"How?" demanded his father, glaring.

"I don't know, but I just know."

Now his mother was offering the firemen and Will cups of tea from a tray she carried. Jasper was still missing, and Jessie was still at Matt's heels. The day had not yet broken, but now that the excitement was over a damp, raw cold seemed to be sinking into Matt's bones, and with it a terrible sadness.

He started to call Jasper again, but his father told him to stop worrying, saying that the dog would turn up and there was no point in waking the whole neighborhood. "It's time you were back in bed," he continued, adding up the cost of the fire in his head and wishing he had never let Jim and Reg have the kitchen units, cursing himself for being weak and changing his mind. "It's the last time that you get anything from us," he shouted to the two men who were now going toward their half-built house.

Jessie heard the anger in his voice and seemed to grow smaller, slinking beside Matt as though she had just committed a dreadful crime, instead of raising the alarm and saving Elijah, Jasper, and the whole barn. But Mr. Painter was too angry to realize that. He now turned to Matt and said, "You did a good job tonight and I'm proud of you, but you're never to speak to those two again. Never! Is that quite clear? If you do, it's good-bye to the dogs. Understand?"

"They came to help. It could have been someone else. It doesn't have to be them who set the barn on fire," Matt said quietly, so quietly that his father hardly heard. "Someone could have done it on purpose. Isn't that what arson is? You haven't any proof, Dad," he added.

"I have plenty. They went in there to fetch those kitchen units they insisted on having. They were smoking when they paid me for them," his father said.

And suddenly Matt was crying, not just over the argument, but because Jasper was still lost and Elijah locked in the woodshed. But most of all he cried because of Jessie, who had raised the alarm and was now cowering at his heels expecting another beating because his father was angry. "I hate this place!" Matt shouted. "I wish we had never come here. Everything's horrid. And you're always angry, Dad."

But his father paid no attention. He strode ahead into the kitchen and then went into his office to write to his lawyers immediately, while the anger was still within him.

"He'll get over it, Matt. He has business worries just now. That's half the problem. But what's the matter with Jessie?" his mother asked.

"She doesn't like him shouting. She thinks she's going to get another beating. You see, she doesn't know what she was beaten for," Matt explained, his face tear-streaked. "Dad's always angry."

"I've just told you that he has business worries. Jessie's been wonderful. She really saved the day. She'll get over the beating," his mother said, pulling his hands from his eyes.

"She won't. She never will. I know it," Matt answered. "And where's Jasper? No one seems to care about little Jasper. You're making tea, Dad's writing letters, and Anne has disappeared. What about Jasper? Are you listening?"

But at that moment Anne came in still in her dressing gown, dragging a reluctant Jasper. "It's all right: I've got him, Matt," she said. "He was standing at the end of the drive. He's a good dog, isn't he? Someone tell him he's good."

So Matt went down on his knees in front of Jasper and told him that he was wonderful. "You were barking, too. You saved us because you woke Jessie up," he said, staring into the dog's restless eyes. Jasper wagged his tail, then started tugging at the piece of string Anne had threaded through his collar. And now the first pale streaks of dawn were easing their way across the sky.

Matt's mother made them all mugs of hot chocolate. "Now it's back to bed," she said.

Matt's father was still typing in his study, his

hands rumpling through his greying hair between letters. And at Willow Cottage a rooster was pronouncing the dawn.

"I can't possibly sleep," said Matt. "And what about Jasper? He can't go back in the barn."

"He'll have to go in the woodshed."

"Elijah's in there already, Mom. There's not room for both of them," said Matt.

"Put him in the old outhouse then. It will only be for an hour or two. Take some straw for him. But let's get the dirt off your face first, dear," said his mother, advancing on Matt with a damp sponge.

Later Matt lay in bed with Jessie lying beside him, trying to sleep. Anne had tried to cheer him up, saying that Jasper was shaping up as a really nice dog, and that his father would soon get over his anger. "In the morning he'll see everything differently," she had said. "Everything's going to be all right, Matt."

But Anne did not know his father as Matt did. How could she? His father had disliked Jim and Reg for a long time, and now he would dislike them even more. He had taken against them from the moment he had seen them. Now, whatever they did, it would always be wrong. When Matt slept he dreamed that Reg and Jim had become rabbits and lived in burrows on the lawn and his father had bought a gun. "Take a look at this," he said, showing the gun to Matt and smiling. "Why do you think I've bought it?"

"To kill the two rabbits on the lawn," Matt answered, trembling in his sleep.

"That's right, clever boy. Then they won't trouble us anymore, will they?"

And now his father looked quite different. He had huge ears and his eyes were Jasper's eyes, only much wilder, and he started to dance saying, "I'll shoot them through the head and then they'll both be dead."

When Matt woke up, he thought for a moment that it was true, and he felt numb all over. Then he saw that it was morning and he slept again.

Six

JESSIE woke Matt up at nine o'clock the next morning and he let her out before returning to bed. Outside everything was dull and murky, the ploughed land stretching away against a dark sky, the trees bare and silent without the whisper of a breeze to stir their branches. Jasper was whining in the old outhouse. Elijah had his head through a woodshed door. Letters were heaped on the front doormat, milk bottles stood by the gate, and a group of ducks were swimming silently in the pond. Jim and Reg were banging away at one of their cars, wool hats on their heads. In the distance Will was wandering up the road toward Willow Tree Farm, hoping to work for a few hours in Mr. Painter's vegetable garden, which was nearly dug.

Before he arrived the Painters were dressed and downstairs, stoking the wood stove, putting the kettle on, upset because the central heating was not yet working. Then Matt opened the back door to let Jessie in and saw a heap of feathers and a note addressed to his father. It was written in capital letters on lined paper, and with a feeling of terror he knew what it would say before he read it.

YOUR DOG HAS DONE IT AGAIN. THIS TIME WE ARE GOING TO THE POLICE.

He knew what it meant—it meant the end of Jessie. Crunching the note up, he found his boots and, calling Jessie, dashed outside.

"Matt, it's time for breakfast. Where are you going?" called his mother, not seeing the feathers.

"Out with Jessie," Matt yelled without looking back, running past Reg and Jim, past Will walking slowly up the drive. He thought, "I'm going somewhere else, but I don't know where. I'm never going back. They won't kill Jessie. She doesn't understand, she can't." He remembered his father saying, "Once she's eaten a chicken, Matt, she'll become a killer. Nothing will cure her then," and now she *was* a killer, because there was nothing but feathers left.

As he ran, he hated his father, Reg and Jim, even his mother, even himself for letting Jessie out. He hated them all because at that moment he was convinced they were all against Jessie. He did not know where he was running. He just ran and he no longer noticed the cold and the water soaking through his boots. He ran as an animal flees from danger, not knowing where he was going, simply fleeing to save Jessie.

Meanwhile his mother scooped up the feathers, crying, "Oh my God!" Anne found the piece of paper and after smoothing it out read out loud, "YOUR

DOG HAS DONE IT AGAIN. THIS TIME WE ARE GOING TO THE POLICE." Mr. Painter could hear her plainly as he entered the kitchen.

"Let me see it. Give it to me. Where's Jessie?" he shouted.

"Gone," Anne said.

"What do you mean—gone?" he asked.

"Matt and Jessie have gone—I think they've run away," Mrs. Painter said, crying silently, clearly upset. "Oh, Maurice, you know how Matt feels about Jessie."

"Why did he let the dog out then?" cried Mr. Painter. "He'll come back when he's hungry. You can be sure of that."

"I'll find him. I'll take Jasper," cried Anne, putting on a raincoat. "I'll bring him back. But only if you promise not to destroy Jessie."

"I won't destroy her, but she'll have to stay on a chain from now on for her own good," said Mr. Painter slowly, looking rougher than usual, because he had not shaved and wore a shirt without a collar. He was reaching the end of his patience.

"You promise then?" Anne asked.

"Yes, but the police will insist that she's kept chained. Tell Matt that. It won't be me that insists— but the police. It's not my fault, but she's a killer."

"Are you going to beat her again, Mr. Painter?" asked Anne, looking at him with steady eyes.

"No, it's too late. We can never cure her now. She's tasted blood, so she'll go on killing. It's a disaster," he said.

"I'll go then." Anne ran outside to put Jessie's lead

on Jasper, who leapt in the air trying to lick her face in a wild demonstration of joy at having been let out at last. Elijah called to her pathetically from the woodshed. Rain was falling now in small persistent drops, the kind which goes on all day. There was no let up in the sullen sky, nothing but grey as far as the eye could see.

At first Matt ran blindly. Then, as the path he had been following took him across one ploughed field to yet another, his legs started to ache and his spirits flagged. He started to wonder where he was going and what he was going to do. "I can't go back and lose Jessie again," he thought miserably, for he was certain that his father would have her killed. Matt imagined him taking her to the nearest vet, saying, "I'm sorry, but she's a killer. We can't keep her." He knew his father too well to hope for anything else.

He reached a low fence and climbed over, helping Jessie over as well. The rain was soaking through his sweater now, and even Jessie was ready to turn back. He found a fallen tree slippery with moss and sat on it. Jessie sat beside him and he put an arm around her. The rain dripped through the trees and gradually the cold penetrated his clothing and his stomach demanded food. The only sound now was the falling rain. Jessie stood up and looked at his face and then gave a sharp bark, then another. She wanted to go back. She did not understand. "You don't want to die, do you? We can't go back, Jessie. Why did you kill the chicken? Why?" Matt shouted at her in despair. "Don't you get enough to eat?" But Jessie did not listen. She kept going away from Matt, then returning. She wanted to go home now and could not understand why they were hiding in the woods. She wanted the warmth of the wood stove or to be in her own basket in Matt's room. She knew nothing of the danger that awaited her there.

Matt was shivering now. Then he heard a voice calling, "Matt. Matt. Wait. Please wait!"

"We had better move on, Jess. Someone's following us," he said. He climbed through a fence to get out of the woods, and Jessie followed. He was in unknown country and he started to run again, sliding down a bank into a ploughed field. He was no longer on a path and all the fields looked the same. There was not a house, road, or even any animals in sight. The rain was sweeping across the open land in a downpour. Jessie did not want to go on, but she followed Matt just the same while the freezing rain beat at their faces and tried to drive them home. There was nothing they could do but go on or turn back, and Matt would not turn back. He was as stubborn and determined as his father, who had often told him, "When you begin something, always finish it, Matt." Now he had begun something, and he must finish it, though how he did not know.

Behind them, Jasper strained on the leash. He could run far faster than Anne and was tireless. Soon Anne's arms and legs were aching and she stopped to call again, "Matt, Matt. Stop! Wait! Everything is going to be all right," and if it had not been for Jasper she would have gone back to Willow Farm then and let Matt's parents find him. But Jasper would not turn back. He was like a hound after a fox. He was following Jessie's scent, and in the damp atmosphere scenting conditions were perfect. And then suddenly Anne could see Matt just beyond a patch of forest, trailing across a field of dark ploughed land with no shelter anywhere and the rain billowing like clouds toward him. "He's being so foolish!" she thought. "I just hope he doesn't hurt himself."

Meanwhile Mr. and Mrs. Painter had taken the car out and were driving around the roads looking for Matt, the windshield wipers working at full speed. They were silent and grim-faced—his father angry, his mother broken-hearted. "You won't kill Jessie, will you?" she asked at last. "You know how Matt feels about her."

"I'm not an ogre. She'll have to stay chained, that's all," he said.

A police car went by, no doubt on its way to Willow Farm. "Perhaps we should move. No one seems happy here," said Matt's mother.

"They're only small troubles," replied Mr. Painter, clenching his teeth.

"Is that all?" asked Mrs. Painter, laughing miserably.

"Yes. That, and the fact that we have two hooligans living almost next door."

"Perhaps you're a little hard on them," Matt's mother suggested quietly.

They had done a full circle now and were back at Willow Farm, but they had not seen a sign of Matt and Jessie. The police car was parked out front.

"He won't stay out long in this weather," said Mr. Painter, getting out of the car. "He'll be back by dinner time. You'll see."

They invited the two policemen inside and promised compensation for the chicken. The policemen were reasonable, only wanting to keep the peace.

"We won't take it further this time, sir, but if she does it again we may have to ask you to have her put down," they said, and put on their caps and left.

"You see, I was right," said Matt's father. "We will have to have Jessie destroyed if she kills again. We can't defy the law, and I'm not begging forgiveness from those two up the lane."

Matt was stumbling now, his boots clogged with mud. Jessie was mud-spattered too, and unable to understand Matt any more. She had thought they were going for a walk, that it was some sort of game. She had tried to tell Matt that it was time to go back, but he would not understand, until at last she simply refused to go another step. Then Matt started to cry and to shout at her like his father and she felt small and humble and afraid, and all the time she could sense that Jasper was behind them. Then they could hear him panting, and Anne calling, "Matt! Please stop, Matt. Don't run away anymore. Please, Matt. Everything's going to be all right!"

Now Matt stood and waited, with the sky opening above him and soaking through everything. He was shivering uncontrollably, with any tears he shed washed away as quickly as they came.

Anne had nearly caught up with him. "It's all right. He's not going to beat her. He's promised," she called.

"What about being destroyed?"

"That, too," Anne said.

Soaked to the skin, Matt looked small and hurt. Anne's raincoat was waterproof so she was still dry underneath, but Matt looked pathetic, obviously on his last leg.

"We had better go back—come on," said Anne, taking Matt's hand. "Otherwise you'll die out here, because there's absolutely nothing, no shelter anywhere. It's horrible."

The woods seemed even wetter this time, the plowed earth heavier. Matt was too miserable to talk, and he felt the pain of defeat gnawing at him. What if his father did not keep his word? Supposing all this had been for nothing? Was Anne telling the truth, he wondered, or was it a trick to make him return home? But he had to trust someone and looking at Anne's face fringed with the raincoat hood, he could see nothing but honesty there. Then he thought, "Dad was wrong about beating Jessie. The beating hasn't cured her at all, and now she will kill again."

Meanwhile Jasper rushed ahead with his tail high over his back, cheerful with success, leading them all home triumphantly. Jessie followed Matt. The rain slowed down, and a crack of light appeared in the dark sky and slowly widened. Pheasants flew upward at their approach. Soon they could see the tall chimneys of Willow Farm.

"Cheer up. Everything's going to be all right," Anne said, smiling at Matt and thinking that her Gran from London would be making coffee now and serving biscuits with it. London seemed a long way from the wet countryside—another world really, she thought.

Will was putting Elijah out when they reached the farm. "Why didn't you take a coat? You are soaked, Matt," he called, as if Matt didn't know.

Mr. and Mrs. Painter were in the kitchen. Jessie slunk past them with her tail between her legs and went straight up the stairs to Matt's room, leaving wet paw marks across the kitchen floor.

Matt's mother said, "Thank goodness you're back, Matt. Come on, dear, let's get your wet things off before you die of cold." Jasper looked at the box of dog biscuits on the kitchen counter and started to bark, while Mrs. Painter ran a bath for Matt. "Don't worry, Matt. Jessie's not going to be destroyed, but the police have been here and it is a worry."

"What's going to happen then?" asked Matt, undressing with difficulty because he was shivering so much.

"She'll have to be kept on a chain, or tied up, that's all."

"On a chain? Jessie on a chain like a criminal?" cried Matt in disbelief.

"It's better than being put down. Oh, Matt, do you think I don't hate it too? And your father, come to that. Be reasonable, Matt," cried his mother.

"It was so lovely when we arrived. Why did everything go wrong?" said Matt.

"It's just a bad patch. We all have bad patches. It will pass and then we'll look back and laugh," his mother said.

But Matt did not believe her. He was not sure he believed anybody anymore.

By the time he had finished his bath, Anne had

dried Jessie with a towel and they went downstairs together to find that Mr. Painter had cooked them a late breakfast of mushrooms, sausages, bacon, and eggs.

"It's what Americans call brunch. Sorry I couldn't manage waffles with maple syrup," he joked.

"But it's fantastic, Mr. Painter!" cried Anne.

He put plates in front of them and served them himself, pretending to be a waiter. Then he put toast on the table and asked them what they wanted to drink. Then he continued, "Matt, you've simply got to keep Jessie on a leash from now on. When Elijah's tethered and you're at school and your mother's working, we can leave her bed in the woodshed and put her on a chain. It will be better than being shut up all day in the house on her own," he said.

"And Jasper? Can't she be with Jasper?" asked Matt.

"Maybe. But one day he's got to find himself a new home."

"I love Jasper. I really do, Mr. Painter," said Anne. "I wish I could have him, but London just wouldn't be big enough for him, would it? Not in Gran's house, and her dog Kim would be upset," she continued. "It's such a shame because he's really nice, Mr. Painter."

"You have been wonderful, Anne, and we are so grateful," he added before turning to Matt to say, "We're going to look at Framlingham Castle this afternoon, so don't disappear again, please. You can bring Jessie along. Tomorrow I'm away again for five days, so you just keep Jessie under lock and key. I trust you, Matt. Okay?"

Anne pushed him with her foot under the table and mouthed "yes" at him so he said, "Okay, Dad. I won't let her kill anything ever again. I promise."

His father patted him on the shoulder before saying, "That's a deal then. Have you had enough to eat?" He cleared away their plates and washed them up, so that Anne was to say afterward, "Your Dad is really great, Matt, whatever you say about him."

In the afternoon they visited Framlingham Castle and Jessie walked the grounds with Matt. As the sky cleared, Matt's gloom lifted. They stopped for tea on the way home. They had left Elijah in the barn so that when they returned they only had Jasper to take for a quick run before giving him his evening meal and shutting him in too. As they passed by Willow Cottage, they saw that all the lights were on. Reg was outside working on a car with a cassette player blaring music into the cold evening air. Matt saw his father's face stiffen with dislike, but he said nothing.

The central heating was working at last. With curtains drawn and the wood stove blazing it felt warm and safe in the old farmhouse.

"It's so nice here—I wish I wasn't going to Holland again tomorrow," said Mr. Painter, pouring boiling water into the teapot. "Make sure Will brings in the coal, and Matt, you're to help your mother. Don't let her do everything," he said.

"Of course we'll help, Mr. Painter," said Anne smiling. "I'll make a cake for you when you get back."

"Only if you want to. You don't have to do the

cooking just because you're a girl," he replied. Matt thought that his father was finally changing, and he realized that all of them were changing all the time.

Everything seemed set fair that evening. They played Scrabble by the wood stove and a wind started to blow from the east, beating against the doors and windows like a devil trying to get in. Jessie whined in her sleep, dreaming that she was with Matt again, traveling further and further from home. Matt watched her, thinking that she did not look like a killer. Her teeth were not for killing, but for carrying. He remembered how often he had walked past the chickens at Willow Cottage with her loose and she had never even looked at them! But Reg and Jim had seen her killing, and they knew her and could recognize her by the snippet of white under her chin. Matt knew that they would not make a mistake, for at one stage they had seemed to love her.

He was very tired now. Twice he nodded off until his mother said, "Matt, you're tired out. Go to bed, love, go on. I'll bring you up a hot drink. Do you want a heating pad?"

He found Jessie's leash and put it on, even though the chickens had long ago gone to sleep in their pen. The wind was like a razor now, cutting against his face and making his teeth ache. "From now on you will always be on the leash, Jessie," he told her sadly. "And there's nothing I can do about it."

His father had repaired the worst of the fire damage to the barn, putting a tarpaulin across the hole in the roof. Soon the man from the insurance would be appearing to assess the damage. Until then, nothing more could be done. But it was not a total wreck, for thanks to Jessie and Reg and Jim's quick action, most of it was still there.

Reg and Jim were in their camper eating a meal, so everything was silent in the drive except for the howling wind. Reg opened the door and called, "Is that you, Matt?"

But Matt did not answer, for he was no longer allowed to speak to Reg and Jim even if he had wanted to. He turned his back on them, pretending not to hear, and went back to the warmth of the farm-house with faithful Jessie in tow, a Jessie who could not understand why she was on a leash.

He found his parents talking about Christmas. "We won't have to buy holly this year, because there's some in our hedge and its loaded with berries. Will says that means a hard winter. We must get a sleigh, Maurice, because I think we're going to need it," his mother said.

Matt imagined snow outside, the trees covered with it, and ice on the pond. Perhaps he would learn to skate. Jessie would like the snow. But what about Jasper? He had never seen snow before.

Anne was missing her Gran and after refusing a hot drink she went to bed. Matt went to bed, too. His mother took him some hot chocolate, and sitting on the only chair in the room said, "Don't ever run away again. You could have died of cold, and think what it did to me and your father. And what did you gain by it? And you did it before when Jessie was a puppy and you thought you couldn't keep her, so this is the second time. Where in the world did you think you were going?"

"I don't know. I didn't think. I just wanted Jessie to stay alive. I was just running. She's my best friend, Mom. Can't you understand? She's always there and she's never angry. I think I would die if I didn't have Jessie."

"Oh Matt, don't say that. There's me and your father too. We care about you. And what about poor Anne? She's not having much of a time, is she?"

"Yes, but you all go away. Anne goes back to London and soon you'll go to work, and you are angry when I'm late for meals. Jessie's always there. I don't mind you getting a job. I don't mind being on my own. I'll like it, as long as I have Jessie. I'm not a baby, and I'm not afraid. It's just that she's company—that's all it is," finished Matt. He gave his empty mug back to his mother and wished he could put what he felt into words, but really his feelings for Jessie defied description. He just knew, come what may, whatever he did, that she would always forgive him. He could think of nothing sadder than having to desert Jessie again, as he had done once before when his father had taken a job in the United States. Now the very thought of leaving Jessie hurt Matt and he had sworn to himself that he would never do it again no matter what happened.

"Stop thinking about Jessie. Think about Anne having to live permanently with her grandmother instead. She hardly ever sees her little brother, because her parents are always abroad. You just don't know how lucky you are, Matt," his mother said, bending to kiss him. "So stop moping, darling. Think of

Anne. She's come for a good time, not for a catalog of misery."

"I'll try, but I'm not making any promises," replied Matt as Mrs. Painter left the room, shutting the door after her before going up to Anne to thank her for bringing Matt back.

Seven

MATT'S father was returning to Holland early the next day. Matt slept soundly and Jessie lay in her own bed beside him snoring gently. He woke at seven-thirty and remembered that his mother would have left to take his father to the airport at six thirty-five. Jessie was whining at the door. He drew back his curtains, which had dogs all over them, not black like Jessie, but white terriers against a brown background. Morning had broken.

Matt ran downstairs with Jessie ahead of him, then put a coat over his pajamas and slipped his bare feet into cold rubber boots. He put a leash on Jessie and opened the back door.

There were feathers there again, a whole heap of them!

It was like a nightmare! Jessie was beside him smelling the air, her nose wrinkling a little. Then she saw the feathers and remembered yesterday. Flabbergasted, Matt let go of her leash, and Jessie's tail vanished between her legs. Then she was gone, loping away while he started to run after her calling, "Jessie, come back. It couldn't have been you, Jessie. It's all right—Jessie, Jes, Jes, Jessie," and Jasper started to bark in the barn.

Reg and Jim were at their gate and, forgetting his father's instructions, Matt shouted, "It wasn't Jessie. I know it wasn't. Not this time."

And Reg called back, "Tell us another, Matt."

Matt found Jessie standing in the road. Her eyes were furtive and anxious and she held up a paw in apology. Her tail was down and she was ready to crawl to him, to beg his forgiveness for something she had never done, and to Matt that seemed the saddest thing of all.

Now he hated Reg and Jim so much that he wanted to call them every awful name he knew. He could no longer bear to talk to them as ordinary neighbors, not ever again. His father was right after all, he thought. They were no good, had never been any good, and Jessie had suffered for it. Then he ran back to the house with Jessie and found Anne on the doorstep reading a note he had not seen.

"Jessie's done it again, Matt," she screamed, her face contorted with rage. "How could you let her? After all your father said! Now she'll have to die and it's all your fault, because you let her out, because you didn't put her on a leash. It's too late now. What's the good of putting a leash on her now? Can't you see, you've signed her death warrant?"

Because she was crying, Matt cried, too. For a moment he could say nothing, for he had never seen Anne like this before. Then he shouted in a stifled voice, "But I didn't let her out, Anne. I promise I didn't! She was in my room."

"What's this letter then?" she shouted back, pushing the scrap of paper into Matt's hand. On it was written, "THIS IS THE LAST TIME. SHE'LL HAVE TO GO."

"But she didn't do it. She was with me, I swear!" cried Matt. "The feathers were there before I let her out, not after!"

"Then I'm going to see those neighbors of yours," Anne said firmly. "Get my coat. Where are my boots? They're not killing Jessie, not while I'm here, or only over my dead body."

"You're still in your pajamas," Matt pointed out, finding her coat.

"I don't care. I'm going now, before they go to the police," Anne insisted, struggling into her coat, her face scarlet with rage and tears. "And you stay with Jessie. Do you hear, Matt? Because you're not allowed to speak to them, remember? But I am," and she ran along the drive, her fair, uncombed hair flying behind her like a flag.

Jessie was trembling all over now. Somehow she knew that she had caused the fuss, that somehow, once again, it was her fault. She wanted to hide somewhere until the storm she had caused had blown over. But Matt was kneeling in front of her now, saying, "It's not your fault, Jessie. It never was your fault. You were beaten for something you didn't do. You don't need to be forgiven, Jessie, not now or ever. You're good, and you always have been good. You must believe me, Jessie." He fetched her dog biscuits, then bread and milk, but she did not want any of it. She only wanted to go upstairs to her basket and hide until her misdeeds, whatever they were, had been forgiven.

Meanwhile Anne banged on the door of the camper where Reg and Jim were having a late breakfast. "You had better come in," said Jim, still unshaven.

Inside was chaos—dirty crocks everywhere and unmade bunks and heaps of dirty washing. "Coffee?" offered Reg.

"No, thank you. Nothing. It wasn't Jessie. That's what I came to tell you. She was inside all the time. It never was Jessie and the sooner you get that in your thick heads the better," Anne said, staring at Jim with burning eyes.

"We saw her," he said. "Mr. Painter must have let her out early before he left."

"You saw another dog," Anne said. "It wasn't Jessie. She was with Matt."

"The first time we saw Jessie carrying Matilda. We took her out of Jessie's mouth. We saw the white under Jessie's chin," Reg said, putting sugar into a mug of coffee. "We are ready to swear to it in a court of law."

"But you didn't see her this morning," cried Anne.

"We saw a black dog, her size and breed. We're not idiots, Anne. We do know Jessie when we see her," Reg said. "And I might add that the Painters have brought it on themselves. We've always been prepared to be friends, but all we've had from them is complaints day in and day out. Let Mr. Painter put that in his pipe and smoke it."

"That's right. We're sick to death of the Painters

and their dogs. I would like to kill Jessie with my own hands, wring her neck—that's how I feel about it just now," Jim shouted. "And if she comes near our chickens again that's what I will do, so you go and tell Mr. Painter that. Go on, and don't come whining back here. What are you doing still in your pajamas, anyway?"

"I'm not whining and I think you are the most awful people I've ever met. I'm not surprised the Painters hate you," cried Anne, stumbling down the camper steps. "And whether I wear my pajamas or not is none of your business!"

"Just tell the old Guv what we've said. Let him put it in his pipe and smoke it," shouted Jim and their laughter followed Anne along the drive, yet all the time she knew that somewhere in what they said there was a clue to something important, something none of them had considered before, something vital.

In the kitchen Matt was sitting with his arm around Jessie. "Well, what did they say?" he asked as Anne entered.

"Nothing much. They laughed and called your father the old Guv. I hate them. They say they saw Jessie carrying the chicken the first time and they saw the white under her chin. But suppose she hadn't killed the chicken? Supposing she was simply retrieving it, Matt? Have you thought of that?" asked Anne slowly. "Supposing something else killed Matilda— the mail van, for instance?" Anne continued, seeing the answer to the clue, seeing Jessie picking up the dead chicken intending it as an offering to Matt. "So now we have to find another black dog. Hurry up,

80

Matt, because there's no time to lose," she finished.

"What about the police?" asked Matt. "We can't just forget them."

"We're not forgetting them. We're fighting. We're going to prove that Jessie is innocent!" cried Anne.

Matt had put the kettle on automatically just like his mother. Now it was filling the kitchen with steam. He made two mugs of coffee while Jessie watched him, hearing her name mentioned, fearing that she was to be sent away again, this time forever.

"We can't prove anything, even if we do find another dog like Jessie. It would never stand up in a court of law, Anne."

"You want to give up, then. Is that it, Matt? You don't care about Jessie?" cried Anne. "You want the police to take her away. Can't you see she's innocent? She's not a killer, she's a retriever. She's bred to pick up dead game and bring it back to you. And that's what she was doing, Matt."

"The first time perhaps, but what about the second and the third time?" argued Matt.

"That's what we're going to find out. We need a tape recorder and a camera. I've got the camera, and your father's got the tape recorder."

"How do you know he has a tape recorder?" asked Matt.

"I've heard him talking into it."

"I can't take it. I'm not allowed in his office," Matt said.

"Well, you can break the rules for Jessie, Matt. Can't you understand? She's like someone waiting to be executed. We're her only hope. For goodness sake, wake up, Matt!" cried Anne, exasperated.

"Okay, I'll get it now, before Mom locks the door like she always does when Dad's away," replied Matt, feeling like a burglar as he hurried through the hall to the old pantry, while Anne rushed upstairs to dress and the morning paper dropped through the letter box onto the hall mat.

A few minutes later they were in the kitchen again, with the tape recorder, which was a small one, in Matt's pocket. Then they heard the car returning and Matt just managed to pick up the feathers and stuff them in the trash can before his mother hurried into the kitchen saying, "I've brought lots of lovely things for breakfast. You're both up early. What's the matter? You look all to pieces, Matt—what's happened?"

"I had a quarrel with Anne, or sort of," said Matt, trying to be truthful.

"You are silly. Quarreling at this time of the morning? I thought you would both still be in bed. Where's Jessie?" his mother asked.

"Upstairs with Anne, I expect, or in my room. She's not outside, anyway," he said, and his heart felt like breaking because he knew where she had gone. She was lying in her basket in his room curled up in the tightest possible ball, her nose under her tail, trying to shut out an unjust world.

"Jessie's killed another chicken, hasn't she, Matt? I can see it on your face," his mother said.

"No. She hasn't," Anne said, coming into the kitchen. "She hasn't killed anything. We know that now, Mrs. Painter."

82

"Can you prove it?"

"We will." Anne had put on a sweater, jeans, and boots. "We are going out to prove it now," she said.

"Well, sit down first and have a croissant, and stop looking like a ghost, Matt. I won't let anyone put Jessie down without good reason," his mother said.

"I hate Reg and Jim. Dad was right about them," said Matt slowly.

"Don't hate, dear. Hate is a poison which eats into you. You must never hate, Matt," said Mrs. Painter.

"I can't stop it. I'm like Dad now. I thought they were my best friends, but I was wrong. They're enemies, dreadful enemies, and they always will be," cried Matt.

It was then that Anne looked at Mrs. Painter and decided to tell the truth. "A chicken was killed this morning, and they still say it's Jessie. They say Matt's Dad let her out before you left in your car. They say they saw her killing the chicken and I think they are ready to swear to it in court. They won't budge," she said.

"Did they see her white patch?" asked Mrs Painter.

"Yes, the first time."

"Did Dad let Jessie out, Mom?" Matt asked.

"No. We were far too rushed for that. She was in your room, Matt, and we left her there."

Anne handed Mrs. Painter the note she had picked up: "THIS IS THE LAST TIME. SHE'LL HAVE TO GO."

Mrs. Painter read it with raised eyebrows. "And you didn't let Jessie off the leash?"

"No, we didn't wake up until after the letter and

feathers had been put by the back door. Jessie was with me sleeping in her basket. Honest, Mom. Cross my heart," Matt replied.

"It's a big mess, isn't it?" she asked next.

Anne was putting on her coat. "Come on, Matt. We are taking both dogs with us. Hurry. I'm sorry about the dishes, Mrs. Painter. We'll do them when we come back," she said.

"Be sensible. Good luck," said Mrs. Painter.

They put both dogs on leashes, and now Jasper dragged Anne along panting and pulling while Jessie walked at Matt's heels trying to make amends for the feathers on the doorstep which seemed to be somehow her fault.

"We'll go to the government housing first. There are dogs there. I've seen them," Anne said.

"Black ones?"

"I can't remember."

"I'm so scared for Jessie," said Matt miserably. "It's worse than a toothache."

"Don't give up—we're winning," Anne said, running on.

They were by the church when a police car cruised by.

"They're going to get Jessie," cried Matt.

"But they can't because she isn't there, Matt. She's with us!" replied Anne, laughing.

"How can you *laugh*?" demanded Matt, who felt like going into the church to pray for Jessie, to ask God to save her, to confess his sins in exchange for her life. But would it be enough, he wondered? Surely God would want more?

They were running automatically, spurred on by the sight of the police car, until they reached the government housing. They were all the same, each pair of houses sharing a dreary concrete path. There were various dogs on chains, but Matt felt sick with disappointment when he saw there was no dog resembling Jessie. Anne gazed in dismay at a large brown dog, then at a funny little golden puppy who was whining against the wire around its pen. "It's so cold for them," she said.

They stood and stared while, inside Matt, hope began to drain away.

"Do you think your mother can stall the police?" asked Anne.

"I don't know. I can't honestly say," and the pain was there again gnawing at his stomach.

"I expect she'll give them cups of tea," Anne said hopefully—as though cups of tea could change a policeman's heart, thought Matt. "Come on, there must be more dogs in the village," she continued, walking on with determination.

But *where?* wondered Matt, and he started to pray as he walked, "God help us save Jessie. Please God, because she's never done anything wrong."

Jasper was still straining ahead and a pale sun was showing its face through the clouds, too pale to light up the sky—rather like a sick person peering through curtains, thought Matt, running to keep up with Anne.

They reached a farm and walked down a lane. Two golden Labradors sat outside a large rambling house. Seeing Matt, Anne, and the two dogs, they rushed forward throwing themselves at Matt's feet, huge golden paws in the air, lips smiling. Then Janet Hinkley, Elijah's former owner appeared, calling, "Hello, what brings you? How's Elijah?"

"Fine. Really lovely, Mrs. Hinkley," called Matt.

"We are looking for a black Labrador as a husband for Jessie," said Anne.

"A husband for Jessie? But it's the wrong time of the year," exclaimed Janet Hinkley.

"For the future. We want to book his services," lied Anne, taking Matt by surprise, making him wonder how she could lie so well.

"Well, I do know of a dog. He's the image of Jessie, except that he hasn't any white under his chin. But I don't really advise his services as he's got such a horrible character—he's locked up most of the day. He's really the nastiest dog I've ever met," Janet told them, stooping to pat Jessie.

"Does he kill things?" asked Matt, his face lighting up.

"Yes, all the time. Absolutely everything—squirrels, cats, rabbits, mice, rats, wild ducks, pheasants, anything and everything," said Janet.

"And chickens?" added Anne.

"Yes, of course."

"Thank you very much!" cried Matt.

"What for? You mustn't let him mate with Jessie—you would have frightful pups. These things are inherited, you know," said Janet. "You don't want a litter of killers, do you?"

"Where does he live?" asked Anne.

"At The Laurels. It's that gloomy house at the

corner—the one which is mostly shuttered. A sad house if there ever was one. But you will only live to regret it," Janet Hinkley called, as Matt and Anne started running, suddenly tireless, their hearts pounding with hope.

Eight

MOST of the curtains were still drawn at The Laurels, but as soon as they opened the garden gate there was an outburst of barking.

"Supposing there's no one home?" asked Matt nervously.

"We'll come back later."

"We can't go home if the police are there waiting for Jessie," said Matt.

"I will go ahead and see how things are, then. Don't be so nervous," Anne said.

"I'm so glad you are here. I don't know how I would have managed without you, I really don't. Jessie would be dead by now," exclaimed Matt.

"Flattery won't get you anywhere," replied Anne, her finger on a polished doorbell.

A woman opened the door. She was still in her bathrobe, and walked with a stick.

"Good morning. We are so sorry to bother you. We are from Willow Farm, and we are looking for a black Labrador dog for breeding purposes," explained Anne and then whispered, "Switch on the tape recorder, Matt. Hurry." He had it in his hand already, hoping that the lady would think it was his radio. His heart was pounding as he pressed the switch.

"Well, we've only got Sinbad. He's a wonderful guard dog and he's got a fine pedigree. He's my son's actually. But Sid's out at work now and I can't speak for him, I'm afraid, but I will pass on your message," said the woman, half closing the door.

"Does he need exercising? We do exercise people's dogs. We don't charge anything. We do it for fun," said Anne frantically.

Sinbad was outside now, growling at Jasper. Sinbad's back hairs stood up along his spine, and he did resemble Jessie to an extraordinary degree.

"My son lets him out every morning before he leaves," the woman continued.

"At about seven-thirty, I suppose?" asked Anne innocently.

"That's right, about seven-thirty, and again in the evening."

"Can we take a photo of him to show to our parents to help them make up their minds?" asked Anne at the same time as Matt asked, "Does he go far in the mornings?"

"Yes, take a picture of him, dear, and let my son have one. I don't know where he goes in the morning, but he's always back for his breakfast at half past eight," she said, quite unconcerned, grey eyes looking at them without interest.

Sinbad was growling now, his lips drawn back showing rows of teeth.

Anne adjusted her camera and pressed the button and there was a flash. "I'll just take another," she said. "You don't mind, do you?" and she pressed the button again.

The woman called Sinbad inside. "I'll speak to my son, then. You did say you came from Willow Farm, didn't you? What's the name?" she asked.

"Painter," Matt said, switching off the tape recorder.

"That's easy to remember. I won't forget, dear," she said.

"I feel awful," said Matt as they walked away. "I hate having to lie."

"It was me who did the lying. And they were all white lies. And I don't regret one of them if it saves darling Jessie's life," Anne said.

"But the son probably loves Sinbad," Matt replied.

"They'll only get a warning the first time," Anne said.

"But it's not the end of the struggle. The police may be waiting for us!" Matt exclaimed.

"We'll play the tape and we'll get the photos developed. We'll ask Janet Hinkley to give evidence because she knows the dog's a killer," Anne argued. "I just hope you pressed the right buttons on the tape recorder. You don't seem very intelligent when it comes to machines."

"I can drive a car," Matt protested.

"An old banger, you mean."

When they reached home the police car was still there, so they hid in the barn and sat discussing the future, worried because they knew that the police car was waiting for Jessie. She lay at Matt's feet while

Jasper wanted to bark and tear around in circles, and had to be held down with a hand over his mouth most of the time.

Anne tried to cheer Matt up. "Everything's going to be all right," she said. "I promise."

"Even though I know Jessie didn't do it, I shall go on being afraid until it's over," Matt said.

"Well, it will have to be over soon because I'm leaving on Saturday, and Wednesday is Christmas," Anne replied.

Matt shuddered, imagining Christmas without Jessie, and no joy in it.

Then they heard the police car go by and, after waiting a minute or two, they crept out into the daylight and ran wildly to the kitchen with both dogs in tow.

"What did they say, Mom?" called Matt.

"Not a lot," admitted his mother, but her worried face belied her words. "They are returning when your Dad is home, and we're going to get a lawyer. We may have to go to court, because as far as I'm concerned we are not pleading guilty which is what the police want," she said wearily.

"Perfect," shouted Anne. "Because we've got the evidence and we'll play it to you in a minute."

"But your father won't wait for the court case. He won't like the publicity. He has to think of his career," Matt's mother continued. "So I can't make any promises."

"He's not having Jessie put down. If he does, I'll run away forever and ever!" cried Matt.

"I'll talk to him. He'll listen to me," said Anne

firmly. "And when he's heard and seen the evidence, he'll know Jessie's innocent and so will Reg and Jim. There's no doubt about it—they can't do otherwise," said Anne. "Then you can all be friends again."

"We'll never be that, if we ever were. There have been too many insults exchanged," replied Mrs. Painter, putting the kettle on.

"And you don't know my Dad like I do, Anne!" exclaimed Matt.

They played the tape. It was rather crackly. The woman's voice sounded whiny and Matt scared, but Anne came over firm and clear.

"It's fantastic. Well done!" cried Mrs. Painter. "It's terrific and I'm so proud of you both, I really am. I feel like opening a bottle of champagne."

"It's not that good," replied Matt.

"I think we should let the police hear it as soon as possible. Where can we get the photos developed?" asked Anne.

Soon they had decided to go into the nearest town that very afternoon and all the anger and the tension evaporated and everything seemed peaceful.

"We're in the clear," said Matt's mother, mixing a pudding. "I think you're just so clever. Perhaps you should go into the police force when you grow up, Anne. Have you thought about it?"

"No. I haven't decided anything yet. I might, I suppose," said Anne, and was suddenly afraid that Matt's mother was being too hopeful about Jessie. Nothing is that easy, she thought. The police could turn up anytime and take Jessie away and break Matt's heart.

When they reached the town it was crowded with Christmas shoppers and no one would develop the film in under three days, and they could not even guarantee that. "It's Christmastime and you know what the postal system is like at this time of the year," said the assistant in the photographer's shop. "I'll do my best, but I'm not making any promises. And you won't get it done any faster elsewhere."

There was nothing else they could do but leave the film, with Matt still saying, "We must have it by Friday, please," and the assistant still insisting that she could make no promises.

After that they did their Christmas shopping, Matt bought his mother a lipstick which took him ages to choose, and a pair of red tights. Then he bought a box of handkerchiefs for his father. He found a book in the second hand bookshop called *Dogs of the World*, which he bought for Anne. Then he returned to the car alone and sat in the back with Jessie, thinking that her days could still be numbered no matter what they did, because the police had asked his mother to plead guilty, which must mean that they had already judged poor Jessie and passed sentence on her. And because his father was unpredictable and would do anything to keep his name out of the local newspapers, there might not be a trial at all.

All the time Matt's heart was crying—there are only four days left until Friday. What if his mother could not manage his father? What if his desk in the old pantry was piled with letters from the police and solicitors all blaming Jessie? Would his father even stop to listen to Matt? Wouldn't he just yell at him for taking the tape recorder, then rip the tape out in a fury? Wouldn't he shout, "That dog has brought nothing but trouble!" Even the photos might not be there in time to prove anything.

All the time Jessie sat with her head on his knee, and people piled cars high with Christmas presents, and the supermarket played *Jingle Bells* over and over again, but Matt wanted only one present for Christmas, and that was Jessie safe for ever.

They drove home, ate crumpets for tea, and took Jasper and Jessie for a walk in the dark. It was freezing everywhere—even the pond was frozen over.

Reg and Jim were revving up a motor bike. Their latest bargain, it would carry them both and save gasoline. It was just one of the economies they were planning for Christmas, along with eating chicken instead of turkey for their Christmas dinner, and not giving any presents. Reg had stopped shaving altogether to save the cost of buying a new brush and soap, and Jim now darned his own socks and mended his boots. They were not bothering about a dessert for Christmas, but they had made some wine and intended to get drunk. They said that they hated Christmas and every time they switched on the radio nothing but Christmas carols were being played. They called Christmas the "annual jamboree" and wished it was over, but really they were sorry they had nothing to look forward to and no one to spend it with. Jim had sent presents to his children who lived with his wife in Australia. Although he pretended otherwise, he missed them every Christmas more than he could possibly say. And Reg missed his mother, who had died two years ago.

The next day Matt, Anne, and his mother brought in holly and pine cones for Christmas decorations and spent all afternoon painting the pine cones red and gold. A heap of Christmas cards had arrived, and although it was still a week to Christmas the feeling of it was everywhere.

Then suddenly it was Wednesday and Matt's father was arriving on Friday from Holland. They were still waiting for the photos to be developed, and an official looking letter had been delivered which might or might not concern Jessie. Matt was very quiet now with a mind full of hate which he could not suppress. And now he knew how his father must feel, for every time he passed Reg or Jim he could feel himself stiffen. He dreamed about Jessie every night—sometimes policemen were dragging her into a police van, sometimes she was declared innocent. This was the worst dream, for Matt would wake in the morning blissfully happy, only to realize that it had been a dream. Nobody could change his mood. Anne tried, his mother tried. Waiting for his father to return, waiting for his decision, waiting for a police car to arrive, all this made Matt feel cold all the time. It killed his appetite and kept him awake half the night. He did not cry, he just wandered about looking, as his mother said, like "a lost soul."

Once he asked his mother, "Do people ever show mercy at Christmastime in memory of Jesus?" But his mother told him that because of Christmas many suspected people might have to stay in custody longer than usual waiting for their cases to come up. Of course that did not apply to Jessie. She would not be in custody because she wasn't human, so her owner would have to go to court in her place. The police would decide that Matt's father was her owner even though he wasn't. Now Matt hated being young. He wanted to be eighteen and make his own decisions, to fight for Jessie like a man and not be a child any longer.

Then on Wednesday night another disaster befell them. The telephone rang and it was Anne's Granny asking her to return. "I have the flu and I need you, Anne. Poor Kim has hardly been out all day, and someone must do the shopping."

Thinking of dear, long-haired Kim, Anne answered, "I understand, Gran. I'll catch a train first thing tomorrow morning. Don't worry. Stay in bed and keep warm. I'll be with you by eleven o'clock. Tell Kim I'll take him out as soon as I arrive. Give him my love."

And Matt stood by the window, thinking, how can I ever cope without Anne? My father won't believe me and the photos are in her name. He couldn't help saying, "How can I manage, Anne? I was relying on you. Why do you have to go?"

"Because Gran has always been wonderful to me, that's why," Anne said, running upstairs to pack.

"But what about Jessie? Don't you care any more?" Matt called up the stairs.

"Of course I care. I shall call you on Friday and you can tell me all about it."

"You know my father won't listen to me, Anne," replied Matt miserably.

"Of course he will. Don't be so afraid, Matt. You really can be a baby," replied Anne, already imagining her grandmother in bed surrounded by medicine, with Kim whining at the door wanting to be let out.

Matt's mother promised to help him. "We'll go in tomorrow and see if the photos are ready," she said, looking at a train timetable. "Don't worry so, Matt. Your father isn't an ogre. He'll understand."

"I wish we could get Janet Hinkley here," Matt said slowly. "I'm sure she would convince him."

"We can keep her in reserve. There's a train at eight-fifteen, will that do?" his mother asked Anne, who had washed her hair and was already moving on to the next thing, which was London and London friends, little Kim, and her grandmother.

"Great! Fantastic!" Anne had brought her hair dryer downstairs with her and was now blow drying her hair, avoiding Matt's eye which seemed to suggest that she was letting him down.

"You'll be all right, Matt, I promise. I know you will. Call me if your father's difficult," she said.

But Matt's father hated him making long-distance calls and was always telling him to write instead of call. Jessie watched Anne with mournful eyes, knowing that she was leaving, while outside the first snow of winter began falling. The next morning it lay, a thin white carpet, over everything.

Anne was up first, her suitcase packed. She breakfasted, wearing her overcoat and gloves. She knelt on the tiled floor to say good-bye to Jessie. The car was a long time starting, but luckily the train was late. Standing on the platform waving good-bye with Jessie at his heels, Matt felt that he was waving hope away. His mother kissed Anne farewell.

"I'll call you on Friday. Be sure to be there," Anne called from the train window, smiling. "About eight o'clock. Is that all right?"

Matt did not answer. He wanted to say something, but was choking back a feeling that Jessie and he had been betrayed. It was not true, of course, but he felt it right down to the core of his being. Anne was leaving just when she was needed most. Her grandmother would not die without her, nor would Kim, but Jessie might.

He waved a hand in farewell and went back to the car with his head down. He could not bear to see the train draw away and with it so much support. He was afraid his mother would take his father's side and say, "It's for the best, Matt. Don't cry," and let Jessie be taken away, never to return. He got into the car with Jessie and shut the door. He refused to speak to his mother. He felt that everyone had let him down and would go on letting him down. If they don't care about Jessie, they could care about *me*, he decided.

The photos were not ready. "Call later. A batch comes in about noon," the same assistant said.

"It's terribly important," Matt said.

"It's out of my hands," the girl replied with a sniff and went to serve another customer.

When they reached Willow Farm again it seemed empty without Anne. Matt took Jasper and Jessie for a long walk. No more snow had fallen, but the whole countryside felt as though it was waiting for it. Now Christmas was less than a week away and tomorrow his father would return, tired from business meetings. He would appear in his business suit and find the official-looking letter on his desk, and Matt's mother would tell him that the police had stopped by about Jessie. He would hear that his tape recorder had been used and he would be angry with Matt. But somehow Matt must convince him that Jessie was innocent. Matt kept rehearsing what he would say, how he would begin, but all the time he was aware that Anne would have put it so much better. He thought of Anne who was now in London, living a different existence, and because of that not caring so much, her concern blunted by distance.

Nine

THE next morning Matt's mother rushed into town to pick up the photos. They showed the black dog clearly, his lips drawn back in a snarl. Matt propped them up on the mantle in the sitting room.

"What do you think, Mom?" he asked.

"Not bad," she said.

"But not very like Jessie," suggested Matt sadly.

"Yes, well, she never looks like that because she's too sweet," his mother said.

He took both dogs for a walk and met Martin. "I'll come around and see you after dinner. I'll bring my cars," Martin said. "Okay?"

"Okay," Matt replied. Martin wasn't Anne, but he was better than nobody. Matt hadn't looked at his toy cars for ages because he felt too old for them, but they would be something to take his mind off Jessie.

Returning home, Matt told his mother Martin would be coming over to visit.

"Fine. He can keep you company while I go to the airport," she said. Every time she mentioned his father or the airport, Matt felt sick, and then his stomach would start gnawing again. Anne would have said "Stop worrying, Matt. I'll manage your father," but his mother was not so certain. She had said that she would take things slowly with his father. Matt had wanted to open the official-looking letter before his father returned. "It may not have anything to do with Jessie for all we know," he told his mother.

"You can't go opening other people's letters. Your father would be furious," she said.

Jessie was worried by the tense atmosphere. She had guessed that it was to do with her and spent every possible moment upstairs in her basket—out of sight, she thought, meant out of trouble. She had the feeling that she was about to be blamed for something and because she felt guilty she would not meet Matt's eye and crept about like a criminal, and that made Matt miserable, too.

The pond was still frozen and the mud was as hard as concrete. Then all of a sudden the weather turned murky, so when Will arrived to bring in the coal and sweep the yard, he said, "It's going to be a bad night. The weather bulletin forecasts fog."

Matt's mother looked worried. "For God's sake stop looking miserable about Jessie, Matt. Can't you see there's a fog coming down? Your father's plane may be grounded," she said.

Matt washed up the lunch dishes. His mother had cleaned the house from top to bottom. Matt had brought Jasper into the kitchen and was trying to improve his manners. Jasper was enthusiastic, and every time he did something right he wanted to lick

Matt's face. He was very quick and anxious to please. It was as though he hoped that if he could do as he was told he would be accepted into the house. But then he would spoil everything by becoming a puppy again and grabbing at tablecloths and tea towels, or picking up someone's boot and racing around the kitchen with it refusing to give it back.

At two o'clock Matt's mother said, "Oh, Matt, can't you see he's hopeless? He'll never learn. He should be a gypsy dog—he's no good in a house. Please take him back to the barn now, before Martin turns up. Otherwise you'll forget and he'll have the place in chaos."

So Matt took Jasper back to the barn and fetched Elijah in out of the cold. He did not take Jessie with him, because in spite of all the evidence he had collected, he still kept her on the leash for fear she would again be accused of something she had not done.

Everything was still murky, with darkness in the air though it was only half past two in the afternoon.

Soon Martin arrived with a bag full of toy cars. Matt rolled up the hall carpet and they raced their cars against each other, writing down the winners on a piece of paper. At half past three his mother brought them glasses of milk and a plate of cookies.

"I have to go to the airport now. I won't be long. I should be back by five o'clock. Will you be all right?" she asked.

"Of course. What do you think? We're not babies," retorted Matt, revving up a Jaguar.

"I'm often left alone. My mom won't mind, Mrs.

Painter," Martin said.

"If I'm late, lock the back door," Mrs. Painter said, clattering down the stairs.

Jessie was in Matt's room, still uneasy, and curled tight in her basket, her nose on one paw, her eyes resigned. A minute later Will opened the back door to call up the stairs, "Well, I'm off now. See you tomorrow."

Normally Matt would have worried about his mother, particularly because fog had been forecast, but he was too involved with his cars, for now the two teams were neck and neck. Finally Martin's team won by three points and they packed up the cars and went to watch television.

At five o'clock Matt started worrying. Jessie was still in her basket and there was something eerie about the way she seemed to know that her life could be hanging in the balance. Matt thought that Jasper did not have the same gift, for he was too busy with living to worry about what might be about to happen. Jasper took things as they came, but like Elijah he had a clock in his head and always knew when a meal was due. At six o'clock exactly he would be expecting his dinner, his mouth watering with anticipation. He would already be whining at the barn door at five minutes to six and Elijah would be looking over the side of the pen Matt's father had made for him, waiting for his evening meal, too. Matt used to sit with them, listening to Elijah's munching, filling up their water buckets if needed. There was something peaceful about Elijah, for though he was strong and obstinate and wanted his own way, he never seemed troubled about anything.

After five o'clock Matt started listening to the sound of the car. He hoped that Martin would stay for awhile, would even take his side over Jessie if need be. But already Martin was saying, "My mom doesn't like me out late. I'd better be going soon."

At ten past five they changed the program on the television, but now even though Matt looked straight at the set, he saw none of it. Instead he saw his father returning, sifting through his mail, still in his overcoat muttering, "What's this then?" and "Not another bill!" And even if the letter was all right, tomorrow would bring the police.

The telephone rang. Matt picked up the receiver. "Hi, Matt, it's Mom. The plane has been diverted, and I've got to go to Stansted. Will you be all right? Is Martin still with you?"

"Yes. Is the fog bad?"

"Yes, awful. I won't be back before nine at the earliest. Do be careful. Lock the doors and don't go out. I wish Anne was still with you. What are you doing now?" Then, because she had no more coins, she was cut off.

"The plane's been diverted to Stansted," Matt said, plonking himself down in one of the armchairs.

"I have to go soon," Martin said. "My mom will be crazed already. She told me to be back before dark."

"Can't you call her?"

"We don't have a phone. We use the one at the estate office in an emergency, and the office will be closed now," Martin said, getting up, finding his coat, and winding a scarf around and around his neck.

Then there was a knock at the door and Martin's father the gamekeeper stood outside, a gun over his shoulder. "Time you were home, Martin," he said, nodding at Matt. When they had gone Matt suddenly felt more lonely than he had ever felt before, so he went upstairs and sat talking to Jessie, and there did not seem to be any sound besides his own voice. I'm not afraid. Why should I be afraid? he asked himself, and did not know the answer. He went downstairs and watched television again.

At five to seven he opened a can of dog meat and called to Jessie, "Come on, Jessie. We are going out to feed Jasper now. Hurry." He put on his coat, boots, and gloves and found a flashlight.

"You don't need a leash because all the beastly chickens are in bed now," he told Jessie as she waited at the door.

The fog seemed to hit him as he stepped outside, wrapping him up as though it were a blanket. Since Jessie's beating he hated fog, and he kept thinking of his mother in it somewhere, car lights on, shut in a small fogbound world—the very thought of it made Matt shiver. He had to struggle to open the barn doors and, once inside, every object seemed to be an enemy waiting to pounce.

Elijah was standing waiting, whiter than the fog. Jasper swallowed his dinner in three huge gulps while Jessie waited in the doorway to go back indoors. The fog seemed to be pouring into the barn through the open door, like a sea invading the earth. At the same time everything was still frozen so that even the water in Elijah's bowl had a thick coating of ice on it.

"All right?" Matt said to no one in particular, before going indoors again to fetch more water because the outside tap was frozen stiff. And now he could hear ducks quacking and the mournful hooting of an owl.

The fog is freezing, he thought, and Mom is out in it, but if the plane has been diverted to Stansted it must mean it's clear in Essex. Now he was frightened for her, too. Anne is calling at eight, but Dad won't be back by then, if he gets back at all, he thought. He will be with Mom, trying to get home.

Matt went back indoors and turned on the television to hear the weather forecast, which was for more cold weather across East Anglia during the night. He put the kettle on, then turned around to speak to Jessie—only Jessie was not there.

He ran upstairs and looked in her basket, but it was empty. He opened the back door and called, "Jessie, Jes, Jessie!" his breath drifting like smoke in the frozen air, but only Jasper howled from the barn in reply.

As he struggled into his boots Matt told himself that Jessie was probably sniffing around somewhere outside. He picked up a flashlight and left the back door open as he tore into the freezing fog, still calling, "Jessie." There was no sign of her anywhere. He decided that he must have shut her in the barn and he flung open the doors, expecting to be greeted by her anxious face, but only Jasper appeared, wildly enthusiastic as usual, his eyes shining in the light of the flashlight. Matt could hear Elijah munching as he slammed the barn doors shut again. Then he ran down to the road to see whether Jessie had been run over by a car. The fog seemed to be moving in front of him as he stood perplexed, his heart hammering, wondering what to do next.

Then he knew—he must make Jasper find Jessie. As he drew near the house he could hear the telephone ringing again, but now it was like something in a bad dream. Let it ring, he thought, for now the only thing which mattered was Jessie.

He seized Jasper by the collar shouting, "Find Jessie, Jasper! Jessie, Jessie, your mother Jessie."

He felt like crying, but some things are too bad even for tears and this was one of them. Jasper was at the edge of the pond barking now and wagging his tail, then running up and down. Terror seemed to be consuming Matt as he shone his flashlight across the ice looking for Jessie. He was shaking, not with cold but with a sort of hopeless fear, and he wished that he was not alone. He wanted someone there to say, "It's all right, Matt. Everything's going to be all right." But there was only Jasper growing more and more frantic with each passing moment.

Then with a sudden rush of hope Matt spotted Jessie's head, which was just above the ice and hardly moving. He shouted, "Jessie. Don't move! I'll get you out. Stay there, Jessie. I'm on my way."

Jessie had not meant to cross the ice. But her nose had told her there was a duck lying dead on it, still warm, and generations of breeding had given her the need to fetch dead game and take it to her master. Nothing could change this instinct. It had made her pick up Matilda the chicken that fateful day, and now it told her to cross the ice and pick up the dying duck and take it to Matt. She scarcely hesitated, as with nose down she stepped on to the frozen pond, and nothing told her that under the far hedge the ice would be thinner because the hedge had given the water shelter. A St. Bernard or a Newfoundland dog might have known this, but not Jessie. As she crossed the ice she was only thinking of the duck, warm and limp in her mouth, an offering to Matt.

Her claws held her steady on the ice and the smell of duck grew stronger, urging her on, so that as she drew near she was moving so quickly that she hardly felt the ice cracking beneath her, then splitting open. Then the water was swallowing her so that she went down and down and then came up, just able to lift her face above the icy water to breathe and smell the air, the smell of home and the smell of duck lying so near and yet so far.

Then she could hear Matt calling her, and Jasper barking, and she struggled frantically, but the ice would not give and she could not climb out of the hole. Matt's voice was louder now and as the beam of his flashlight lit up her face he shouted, "Take it easy, Jessie. Don't move!"

He tried standing on the ice, but almost at once it started to crack beneath him and a nagging pain joined the feeling of sickness which had been with him all day. He shouted, "Help, help! Jessie's trapped. Help!" and the fog caught his voice and stifled it.

He ran to the barn for a piece of rope, but there was not a piece long enough to reach Jessie, and the beating of his heart seemed to be racing in his ears faster than an express train. He found a ladder and carried it to the pond, but it was not long enough either and all the time Jessie was still paddling, with her body temperature falling.

Then Matt cried to God to please help him, while Jasper ran tirelessly up and down the edge of the pond, barking encouragement to Jessie, and her limbs grew cold, so cold that at times they stopped moving altogether. Matt ran to the road to see whether his parents were approaching, but everything was silent and deserted.

He ran quickly back and stood outside Willow Cottage, not daring to knock, praying that someone would appear, but no one did. When he returned to the pond Jessie's head was hardly visible anymore. Though she could hear him calling and wanted so much to reach him, her strength was leaving her now, and she was so cold that sometimes she almost slipped beneath the ice to disappear forever.

Fifteen minutes had passed now and in all that time Matt had achieved nothing. He had called on God, and God had not answered. He had looked for his parents and tried to find a ladder or a rope long enough to reach Jessie. Now there was only one thing left he could do, and that was to go back to Willow Cottage and ask for help. During the few minutes it took him to reach its doors, he heard his father's voice telling him never to speak to Reg and Jim again, and Anne telling him that Jim wanted to strangle Jessie with his own hands, and all the other terrible things which had been said. They were like something around his throat, choking him. Then he remembered his mother saying, "It's the things you don't do in life that you regret, not the things you do." Then he was banging on the door, banging and shouting, "Help! Help! Come out please. Please save Jessie," he prayed as he began to cry. "She's fallen through the ice—*please*," not noticing the tears suddenly cascading down his face.

Reg and Jim had only moved into the cottage that day and were celebrating, sitting with their feet up and drinking beer. "There's someone banging. What can anyone want on a night like this?" cried Reg, going to the door in his socks and shooting back the bolts, while Jim switched off the television.

To Matt standing outside it seemed to take an age for the door to open. Then staring at Reg, he screamed, "Jessie's fallen through the ice, and she's drowning. Please help, please. You must help me save her!"

"Right. Hang on," cried Reg, seizing his boots, while Jim found a flashlight and asked, "In the old horse pond? How long ago?"

"I don't know, ages—twenty minutes at least. She'll give up in a minute, I know she will," screamed Matt.

Then Jim said a strange thing for a man who had talked about strangling Jessie a few days ago. He said "Poor little thing. We'll get her out somehow, don't you worry. You should have come straight to us."

"I know, and she may be dead already," Matt said.

"Where's the Guv then?" asked Jim next, switching on the car headlights, then starting the engine and driving to the pond with Matt running behind with Reg. Now they could all see Jessie clearly in the light from the headlights. Her small pathetic head was still above the ice, but only just. Matt started to shout again, "Hang on, Jessie. Don't give up." Her head disappeared altogether, then came up again. She was nearly at her last breath now, struggling for survival, barely conscious, ready to let go. Only Matt's voice was giving her the strength to go on fighting.

"I know! The canoe, Reg—the old canoe!" shouted Jim, and then the two men were running back toward the cottage. Jasper was still barking, growing hoarser all the time, telling his mother not to give up, jumping on and off the ice. But now Jessie was giving up, her whole body was weakening. She had been swimming now for nearly thirty minutes and she could no longer hear Matt or Jasper. A feeling of warmth was stealing over her, loosening her limbs, and she was ready to let go, to give up, to go to wherever dogs go when they die.

The two men threw the canoe onto the ice, and Reg leapt in because he was the lighter. He pushed out with paddles, muttering, "I hope it's watertight. I don't want to drown just before Christmas."

There was a sound of breaking ice. Matt could not bear to look anymore. Some sixth sense had told him that Jessie had given up. Jasper had stopped barking and was returning to Matt with a look on his face which seemed to say, "It's all over. We needn't bark any more."

Matt stood by the pond in despair. All the struggle over the last few days to prove Jessie innocent now seemed futile. He knew his mother would make the best of her death. She would call it fate, and "You can't fight fate," she would say. "You did your best, Matt. Nobody can do more than that, love."

But Matt knew that it was not fate. It was his fault for not keeping an eye on Jessie, and it would remain so until his dying day. His father would promise him another dog, one that he could show this time, with no snip of white on its chin to prove that somewhere in its ancestry there had been a mongrel. But Matt did not want another dog, because there would never be another Jessie. He would make do with Jasper, now whining pitifully beside him. Jasper, too, had done his best, but he would get over Jessie dying, thought Matt, because he was a dog who could endure anything. As for Matt, he did not want the sun to rise on another day and did not want to go on at all without Jessie.

Then Reg cried, "I've got her, but I don't know whether she's dead or alive," and Matt could see that he was lifting something into the canoe, something black and silent and covered in pond water, and his heart cried, "Jessie, don't give up."

Jim threw a rope across to Reg. "Ready. Heave ho!" he cried. Jasper was barking once more and running up and down the bank, his eyes alight with hope. Matt could hear the telephone ringing in the house again, but he did not move. He just waited, frozen with fear, to see whether Jessie was alive or dead.

Ten

THEY laid Jessie down by the pond and Jim bent over her, pushing on her chest. "I can't feel anything. I think she's gone," he said. Jasper stood silently watching. Matt could not speak, so great was his anguish. Jim held poor Jessie up by her hind legs and let the water stream out of her nose, then put his ear to her side and said, "There's just a flicker of life. Fetch something warm to wrap her in, Matt. Hurry! Don't stand there gawking."

Matt ran as he had never run before, straight into the kitchen and up the stairs. Ignoring the still ringing telephone, he snatched his bedspread and in three leaps was down the stairs and rushing back to the pond.

"Good boy. She's still breathing, but only just. Pity you brought something nice like this," Jim said, laying her gently in the bedspread. An old rug would have been better. Your Mom will never forgive you."

"I don't care. It's the warmest thing I've got," cried Matt.

They laid Jessie on the backseat of the car. "You

sit with her, Matt, because she knows you. Cuddle up to her to keep her warm," Jim said.

"Where are we going?" asked Matt, climbing in beside Jessie, who was lying utterly still, with evil-smelling pond water dripping through the bedspread onto the floor of the car.

"To the vet," said Jim.

Reg leapt into the driver's seat and, swinging the car around, skidded wildly as they tore down the drive. Matt realized with surprise that he and Jim were risking their lives to save Jessie, as well as using their last drop of gas. He was so grateful that he felt like crying. Their breath froze on the windows and the fog was so thick that they could only see a few yards in front of them, but Reg drove as though the sun was shining. "Is she still breathing, Matt?" he shouted as they reached the main road.

"I think so."

"Talk to her—she needs you," he said.

So Matt said, "You're going to be all right, Jessie. You're not drowning any more. You're safe and I'm here," and through the bedspread he could feel her breathing becoming stronger, though it was not normal, being fast one moment and desperately slow the next. It was the sort of breathing which could stop at any time, running down like a clock, then stopping forever, thought Matt. The sound of it both pleased and terrified him. It pleased him because it meant she was alive and terrified him because at times it was so faint and feeble that he feared it would stop altogether.

Then, like a miracle, the fog lifted. One moment

114

it was there, the next they could see hedges on both sides of the road and houses lit up, twinkling with Christmas tree lights. There were people going into a bar, and street lamps glowing warmly. It was rather like coming out of night into day, or from a tunnel into light.

"Does the vet have evening hours?" asked Jim.

"I have no idea," said Reg.

And this was another new worry, for what would they do if everything was locked up, if there was no one to help them? Matt could not bear to think about it.

"They must have an emergency bell," said Jim.

"Of course they do," agreed Reg.

Matt wondered whether they were saying it just to soothe him. His parents had often done that in the past, saying things like, "You'll be better in the morning, love," and "You'll grow to like school, I know you will," and they had often been wrong.

Now they had reached the vet's clinic and all the lights were on and there was still a car in the parking lot. They all felt like cheering as Jim lifted a limp Jessie out of the car and carried her swiftly to the surgery door, and at that moment the two men seemed the best friends Matt had ever had.

There was an elderly woman in the waiting room holding a large ginger cat on her knee and she looked at them and said, "I'm next—you'll have to wait."

"We can't—it's a life and death case," shouted Jim and carried Jessie straight into a room with "J. Mercer" on the door.

"She's been drowned in a pond. We need help and

quickly," he said.

"She fell through the ice. I couldn't get her out. I think she's dying," said Matt miserably, still shivering, half from cold, half from fear.

Jim laid her on a table and Joan Mercer, the vet, unwrapped poor Jessie while they stood in silence waiting to hear what she would say. To Matt, looking at Jessie, who seemed so much smaller and thinner because she was wet, it seemed the longest moment of his life.

"She's still breathing. Warmth is the important thing. I'm going to wrap her in the latest invention for hypothermia. It's part tin foil, part polyester," said Joan Mercer, turning toward a cupboard.

"Do you think she will live?" asked Matt in a voice cracking with emotion.

"I think she's got a fighting chance. How long was she in the water?" asked Joan Mercer, who was as thin as a bean pole with red hair.

"Twenty minutes or longer," Matt said, as the vet dabbed at Jessie with paper towels, trying to get rid of the worst of the pond water before wrapping her in the special silvery blanket. Then she found a tartan rug and put it over the top.

"I can't promise she'll live," she said, looking at Matt with steady blue eyes. "She'll be best at home by a warm fire with hot water bottles in her basket— not too hot though, just bearable on the back of your hand. She may get pneumonia, or her lungs may be affected. If she gets worse, call me. Otherwise I'll be around tomorrow. You've ruined the bedspread, but never mind, it may have saved her life. Now, can I have your name and address, please?"

A minute later, Jim was carrying Jessie out of the clinic. The elderly woman was still there in the waiting room with the large ginger cat on her knee. She glared at them and muttered, "You've got some nerve, I must say." No one answered.

Matt's parents were home now. For the last part of their journey the skies had been clear and the driving easy, but they were both very tired. They stared at the canoe left in the pond and saw that Jasper was loose. Then they discovered, in total disbelief and horror, the open back door. Then Mrs. Painter was shouting, "Matt! Where are you? Oh, Maurice, I knew something was wrong when he didn't answer the phone. Oh, why did I leave him? He's drowned in the pond! Look over there—there's a hole in the ice. I said something terrible had happened, Maurice, I told you!"

"Don't jump to conclusions," cried Mr. Painter, running toward the house and calling, "Matt, are you all right? Answer me, Matt. It's your father."

But there was no answer and no comforting message on the table in the living room to explain Matt's absence, just dirty foot marks all over the kitchen floor and two dirty mugs in the sink.

"I thought Martin was staying. I thought they would be all right together," sobbed Mrs. Painter while Jasper ran around them barking wildly, trying to tell them what had happened.

"Where's Jessie? He must have gone in after Jessie. Perhaps we should try the pond first," cried Mr. Painter.

"Or call the police," replied Mrs. Painter going upstairs, seeing that Matt's bedspread was missing. "His bedspread is gone. He must be wrapped in it somewhere. Oh my God, we had better call the hospital. I'll do it while you look in the pond, Maurice," she cried, clattering down the stairs.

As Jim laid Jessie on the backseat of the car, Matt thought he saw her tail moving. He sat beside her, holding her head on his knee.

"You had better come to our place and have a spot of tea," said Jim kindly. "You look worn out."

Matt looked at the two men. Their faces looked the same as they had always looked—perhaps a fraction happier because they liked emergencies and being useful, but otherwise unchanged. They did not seem to be the men his father hated. Rather, they seemed kindness itself.

"No, I must take Jessie home, thanks all the same. But I thought you hated her," he said.

"Oh, no. We don't hate her. It wasn't Jessie who killed the chickens. It was that dog at The Laurels," Jim said smoothly, starting the car.

"But . . ." began Matt.

"We only discovered it a day or two ago, the day you went shopping with Anne and your Mom. We caught the dog in the act and followed him home. He had slipped out of his collar, you see," explained Jim.

"Why didn't you tell us then?" asked Matt. "Why?"

"We wanted the Guv to sweat a bit, that's why. We never set fire to the barn. If it was anyone it was the plumbers going in there to eat their dinner. It was never us, but try telling that to the Guv."

"I wish you wouldn't call him the Guv," Matt said. "Why don't you call him Maurice?"

"He wouldn't like that, not the Guv," replied Reg.

"How do you know? You haven't tried," Matt said.

The sky had cleared and they could see stars like lights in the sky. Matt could feel Jessie breathing now, steadily like a clock.

"I wish you had told us you knew about the other dog. I've been so miserable. Have you told the police?" he asked.

"Yes. And they won't be calling on you again," Reg said.

"I wish you had told us," repeated Matt.

"We would have. We were biding our time," Jim said.

They were home now and the familiar car was parked outside Willow Farm. Matt's father was standing by it with a flashlight in his hand.

"Where have you been?" he shouted.

Another second and Matt's mother was flying out of the house crying, "Matt, are you all right? What happened? We kept calling and then when we arrived you weren't here. We've called the police and the hospital. We were just going to start a search. Why didn't you leave a note?"

"There wasn't time," replied Matt, and now Jim was standing behind him holding Jessie in his arms, with only her nose showing from under the rug.

"Where do you want to put her, Mrs. Painter?" he asked, while Jasper ran around and around Matt in circles of joy.

They laid Jessie by the wood stove. "Reg and Jim

saved her, Dad," Matt said quickly. "She would be dead if they hadn't helped, and they know she didn't kill the chickens. And it was the plumbers who set fire to the barn—it must have been." He was talking far too fast because he was afraid that his father was about to dismiss Reg and Jim without saying thank you. He was afraid they would still be enemies, and now that they had rescued Jessie he could never be their enemy, however much his father wanted it. He moved over to stand beside his parents, looking at his mother and begging her help with his eyes

"This deserves some discussion. Sit down," said Mr. Painter, waving Jim and Reg toward two chairs. "I think we all need some refreshment."

"The police know it wasn't Jessie, so they won't be turning up again," said Matt, kneeling beside Jessie to watch her breathing. Her eyes looked at him now as though she was returning from a long sleep, and her tail began moving gently beneath the rug.

Matt filled two hot water bottles, testing them on the back of his hand as the vet had told him, before slipping them into the basket which his Mom had fetched for Jessie from upstairs. All the time Reg and Jim were talking to Mr. Painter, who presently said, "I just want to thank you both. There have been faults on both sides, but all that is over now," and held out his hand.

The two men shook his hand saying, "Okay, Guv," and Jim said, "Not Guv, it's Maurice from now on."

Next they shook Mrs. Painter's hand, while Jasper sat by the wood stove making himself quite at home, though usually he would have been sent to the barn by now.

After that they discussed running a business, and Matt's mother had told them about *Just Your Luck*. "We're opening on New Year's Day," she said.

"Perhaps we could help you with transport," suggested Jim tentatively, while Reg, embarrassed, turned his wool hat around and around in his hands.

"Yes, that's quite an idea. Not at first, because to begin with we can manage with my friend Candy's station wagon. But as we grow we may need you," said Mrs. Painter.

"We could do light moving as well. What do you say, Maurice?" asked Jim.

"You'll have to get permission from the County Council to run a business, but I won't stand in your way," said Mr. Painter.

"Yes, we'll do that, then."

"There are still grants for small businesses, I believe," continued Mr. Painter.

And now the kitchen felt full of hope. Looking at his parents with Jim and Reg, all talking together, it seemed like a miracle to Matt. But then as his mother was to say later, "Christmas is a time of goodwill. A time to let bygones be bygones." And even as they talked they could hear the distant sound of carol singers singing *The First Noel*.

"I know we started off on the wrong foot," Jim said, "But it wasn't meant, Maurice—none of it was meant."

And Mr. Painter, still remembering the moment when he thought that Matt might be dead, said, "It was all out of proportion. I was too finicky. I see that now."

"We won't be getting any more old cars, not if we're going into the moving business," Jim said. "We'll make a parking space at the side of the cottage. The moving van won't be in the driveway."

Matt listened, hardly able to believe his ears. Then the telephone rang and he rushed into the living room and picked up the receiver. It was Anne.

"What's happened? I've been calling and calling. Where have you been? I've been so worried. Has your father heard the tape yet?" she asked.

"It doesn't matter," Matt said. "We're all friends now. It's very strange. I never thought it would happen. I still can't believe it. And Jessie is still alive, but only just. It's a really long story," Matt related and his voice sounded slow and very tired to Anne in London. "Reg and Jim saved her," he continued. "I'll write and tell you all about it. They know she didn't kill the chickens. They've known for some time. You were right—she must have picked up Matilda when she was already dead, killed by the mail van perhaps, but we'll never know for sure what killed her. I can't believe that Dad is friends with them now, it's such a change. But I think Jessie is going to live." He was rambling now, and so tired that his voice sounded slurred. "Mom and Dad got lost in the fog. I was on my own, and I couldn't get Jessie out of the ice. Reg and Jim saved her, Anne, and took her to the vet and did everything. Do you think everyone will stay friends, Anne?"

"I don't know. Your father is so moody and they

sound crazy. I think you're all a little crazy," Anne answered, feeling safe and peaceful in her Gran's elegant sitting room.

"Reg and Jim are going to start a moving business. Thank you for everything, Anne. I must go now. I'll write soon. Good-bye," finished Matt, putting down the receiver and going back to the kitchen. Someone had unwrapped Jessie, and she looked almost normal now. She wagged her tail and raised her head and looked at Matt with eyes full of devotion.

Mr. Painter was inviting the two men over to have Christmas dinner.

"We'll bring some of our own wine," said Reg.

"And a big piece of cheese," added Jim.

"That will be fine," said Mr. Painter.

It seemed an extraordinary end to a terrible day, thought Matt, as Mr. Painter looked at him and surprisingly winked. And Matt could see Christmas now in his imagination—Jessie completely recovered, Jasper sitting quietly, all of them feasting. They would raise their glasses to eternal friendship, and all because Jessie had fallen through the ice. It had taken that to end the hate between them, but then, as Matt's mother was to say later, "It's an ill wind which blows nobody any good."

As for Jessie, she lay down again and sighed, and the sigh said, "It's good to be home and to know everything is all right." A feeling of peace enveloped her as she drifted into an exhausted slumber. Without ducks on ice, or unexpected beatings to haunt her contented, dreamless sleep, she awoke in the morning completely recovered and ready as always to spend the whole day with her beloved Matt.

About the Author

Christine Pullein-Thompson has written children's stories for over 40 years. Born in Surrey, England, in 1930, she writes about animals surviving in the wild, raising ponies in the countryside, and hunting with woodland foxhounds.

At about age 15, Pullein-Thompson wrote her first book with her two sisters. Most of her stories have been about ponies.

Now she is director of a riding school. When she finds time, she writes children's books from her home in Suffolk, England, where she lives with her family, ponies, cats, dogs, and hens.